THE BOUNDED CURSE
By Ana Stanojevic

2024

The characters and events in this book are fictional. Any similarity to real persons, living or dead, is coincidence and not intended by the author.

Stanojevic, Ana

The Bounded Curse

Under a Federal Liberal Government, library and Archives of Canada no longer provides Cataloguing in Publication (CIP) data for independently published books.

To those who believe in magic

CHAPTER ONE

IN THE LAND OF MAGIC

Tinkle! Crackle! Sizzle!

Sounds burst into the open sky, filling it with different colors as if they were almost creating a firework show. They tore across the dark expanse, showing flashes of different harmonized colors. But then a second after, it all grew subdued, going quiet. Every once in a while, it showed up again, but from a different spot each time, appearing and then dying only to reappear again.

The City Grand Centre was certainly full today. Crowds upon crowds strolled through the busy streets. Most of them carried heavy bags with both arms while some were using their magic as they didn't want to bother carrying them. A few passengers nearby sat on the benches at the side of the hectic street, either chattering or watching the small magic shows emitting from different shops around the area. Occasionally, there'd be a popping sound, but within seconds, a man appeared as though he'd conjured a vortex to get to the spot where he needed to be. He adjusted his trench coat collar before going on his way.

The Grand Centre was quite a huge area with skyscrapers to the side, stacked level upon level, all colored either brown or white. Some circular buildings were also scattered across in different places. A few of the streets narrowed down to small sidewalks while in the middle ran tracks for the trolley train.

The train zoomed past by the citizens every now and then, ringing its bell to alert the people. Passages were split in two at the wide, V-shaped beige building which stood in its way, going in different sections, leading somewhere else off the Grand Centre—possibly to the next shopping area or street markets.

Another passageway seemed to be going more uphill, away from the Grand Centre. The shops, however—filled with chatter from the people—were mostly located in the main area. All of the stores took the form of different shapes: circular, rectangles, triangles, all of them lined up beside each other. One store even took the shape of a tall tower with its roof slanted forward, making a dip. However, there seemed to be some kind of magic surrounding the front, supporting it so it wouldn't collapse.

Each of them was as busy as the next, the customers either browsing or waiting in line to pay for their latest purchase even though it seemed to last forever as the lines were quite busy. The workers quickly rang the customers' transaction to the best they could, trying to keep them happy since they knew the lines were incredibly hectic and long.

"You don't want this?" the worker asked, showing the item to the customer.

"Yes, that's right. I seem to have changed my mind about it."

Nodding, the worker tapped on the box, and in a second, it disappeared in a puff of smoke.

The other workers on the floor were busy with the customers, trying to keep up with their orders, constantly going to the back to get their requests, and there were times a worker didn't have what the customer wanted.

"You don't have this anymore in the back?" a shopper—short and plump with a pointed nose, frilly grey hair, and bearing an elderly look—pursed her lips in disappointment.

"N—no. I'm sorry," the helper stammered. "However, if you wish, I can place an express order for you."

"No. No, that would be quite alright."

"I'm sorry."

Another store, which was medium-sized, was filled with different robes for all occasions. Most of the robes were hung for display, on the mannequins or at the window, seemingly floating. Straight ahead would be the fitting area where two workers were adjusting the robes for the customers. Inside the shops, there would be brooms floating by themselves as they cleaned the floors from all the dust and the fabrics of the robes.

"No, no! I didn't want it to be cut *that* small. Now, the bottom of my ankles will be shown!" a customer said, exasperated. "And please adjust the collar, as well. It's really irritating my neck."

Usually, the shoppers would be so busy, they wouldn't even notice how quickly the time had passed. A large clock, planted on the tall column of a building, made a loud *dong*, echoing its ring across the city.

"My goodness! Is it four o'clock already? My, how the time passes by so quickly!" a citizen exclaimed, eyes wide. He then scurried hurriedly going down his path.

Even if the time went by fast and night had fallen, the streets would still be crowded. There would always be some kind of attraction in the city's centre where many crowds would have been gathered to see the latest show, applauding in the right spots. Other crowds would be walking down the streets, taking a moonlight stroll where the moon would shine its eerie rays, illuminating the city with its powerful glow. As the clock struck midnight, the once-crowded streets would grow subdued with silence as the citizens made their way to their homes, done for today.

And so the day would always go. The routine would always be the same. Eat. Sleep. Wake up. Go to work. And repeat.

Morning came, and where the sky used to be covered in blackness, it was now filled with bright rays from the morning sun. The rays would stretch on forever as the sun rose up until it finally shrugged itself out of its deep slumber.

Everyone woke up again, ready to start their repetitive business as usual. The Centre began to grow crowded once more, and the once-closed shops would now reopen, ready to start the day and get on with business. Ready to have their interiors packed.

However, in the middle of the huge centre stood a fountain that began to come alive, sprouting out its glittering water. And beside the fountain ledge stood a boy, aged twenty, who appeared to be of medium height, with slightly spikey black hair and dark tan skin. His captivating black eyes stared ahead, watching the crowd like how a lion watched its prey before it attacked. His face was sharp all around: sharp nose, sharp jaw, with slightly sharp cheekbones.

He was somewhat built with muscles in the arms and had broad shoulders with a lean body. He wore a black, slightly loose elbow-sleeved shirt with beige pants and white sneakers.

Regardless of the beautiful scene before him, he was bored, and he wanted nothing more than for those two who'd accompanied him to hurry up. He hated shopping and would never enjoy it *but* maybe to some extent. Only if shopping wasn't so...*girly*. He often wondered how Bastein dealt with it.

"Cain!" a loud voice yelled over the crowded streets.

He was surprised he'd even heard the call, and he turned around only to see his friend poking his head out of the door, waving his hand at him to indicate he was supposed to come.

Cain groaned. With reluctance, he grudgingly walked towards the small, narrow shop.

"What?" he asked, annoyed.

Bastein smirked.

"No need to look so happy," the skinny boy, aged twenty-one, with dark brown hair that almost covered his grey eyes, drawled. He had soft cheeks and small ears, with a softly shaped jaw. He wore a plain baby blue T-shirt with black pants and pull-top sneakers.

"Piss off," Cain muttered.

He squeezed himself through the door after Bastein had disappeared. Inside, the shop was extremely crowded, but it looked wider than it seemed outside. Outside the store was a medium-sized window with posters covering it up.

Have you ever wished you can be so full of energy? To never be drained? Come check out our new spell! It's selling out fast!

Inside, the ceiling was high and slanted, almost like in the shape of a triangle. Shades of blue, yellow, pink, orange—every different kind of colors of magic—were visible as they had all been thrown in the air because of the customers trying out different spells. On the upper level that had a balcony at the top of its stairs, there was also a small stand full of books. Most of them were on how to properly conjure a spell or how to channel your energy with the spell and the basics and so on.

The helpers were scurrying all over the place, assisting the shoppers while at the same time trying to cancel out the spells before things got too hectic.

Cain swerved to the side as a yellow spell slithered past him, hitting a wall and leaving a scorching mark. Frustrated, the worker pointed his finger at the burn, and a white, almost invisible streak of magic appeared, causing the mark to instantly vanish.

Bastein ducked down to dodge an orangey spell that flew his way. Eventually, after pushing through the crowd, the two finally met up with their third friend who was too busy to even notice them as she was trying out different spells. But her pale body was being illuminated by the colors from the magic she was conjuring.

"Releasis!" the twenty-two-year-old blond-haired female with green eyes said. She had smooth cheeks on an oval-shaped face and wore a black, long-sleeved turtle-neck shirt with black leggings and a checkered plaid skirt. She also wore black flats to complete the look and had her hair in two braids. A thin silver chain stuck out of her shirt and showed an hour-glass pendant filled with an amethyst color. Freckles were liberally dusted across her low cheekbones.

A shade of purple got released from the jar she was pointing at. But this one went to the side, and it nearly struck Bastein and Cain who avoided it just in time. However, an irritated worker flickered his hand to cancel out the power before it could do any damage.

"Have you ever thought of buying a spell that would improve your aim?" Cain asked.

The girl turned around and saw the two boys though she rolled her eyes at Cain's remark. "Whatever."

Bastein eyed the many spells—contained in jars—she was holding in her hands. "And are you trying to buy the whole store or something?"

"No. I'm trying out different ones, but I'm thinking of getting the new spell everyone's raving about. In case you haven't noticed, the store just released a new enchantment, which is why it's so busy."

"We noticed," Cain replied.

"Hmph. Could've fooled me. You aren't very observant." The female friend smirked.

Cain growled, clenching his fists. "If you're done buying, can we go?"

She rolled her eyes. "Sometimes, I think we should've gone to a potion shop to buy you a mood potion. You're always so moody."

Cain rolled his eyes before he stalked out of the store.

"Case in point," she said simply.

Bastein took this time to examine all the colorful jars containing liquids or floating mists placed on the shelves stretching almost to the ceiling. There really was *a lot* of variety of enchantments in here. From simple spells to advanced. He wondered if the store contained forbidden spells—not that he would ever need one or wanted to have one.

"Okay," she announced. "I've made my decision. We can go pay."

In all honesty, Bastein was *glad* to finally hear those words. He didn't think it was possible to spend *three hours* in a shop, although sometimes, it felt like it was more than three hours. That being said, he pitied the workers who had to clean up the mess, during or after hours as the enchantments could get nasty and out of control, to the point where even the manager of the store had to come in and take care of everything.

"Twenty-five dinars," the cashier said.

The girl paid the money and grabbed her bag and walked out of the store, Bastein following her shortly.

"Avery's done? Unbelievable," Cain said after seeing them coming out.

"Unlike you, I got new spells to try out," she responded.

Cain shrugged. "Like I could care."

"You never care about anything," she muttered.

Bastein sighed as he was racking his brain for a spell that could potentially heal the rift between the two. They'd been at each other's throat since the day they'd met. Even though he couldn't think of a spell, something else did come to mind where he was sure even the two would actually agree on something.

"Hey. I got an idea," he suddenly said. "If we're done shopping here, why don't we spend the day at the Warlord Wakeley?"

Avery gasped. "Bastein, that's a fantastic idea. I always liked going there. Especially with my parents."

Bastein tried to ignore the bitter tone that fell from Avery's tongue when she mentioned her parents

Cain nodded. "That sounds like a plan."

"Great, then. Let's get going now. I don't feel like waiting for an hour just for the train to come," Bastein said.

CHAPTER TWO

WARLORD WAKELEY

"Thank you," Bastein muttered as he took the tickets from the ticket booth.

The employee nodded and glanced at the customer behind him. "Next, please!"

A sign hanging from the side of the ticket booth read: EDGESHADE.

A loud whistle was heard from the distance before, finally, from around the corner appeared a huge red train with multiple carriages, all packed with people. Most of the passengers on the train got off, ready to head to whatever destination they needed to go. The red walls of the large train glistened brightly, showing off the glamorous look of what the vehicle held.

"Alright, go on. We're in second class," Bastein said as he got into the carriages.

"Oohh, look at you going all in." Avery grinned.

"The next time we do this, you can pay. And I promise I won't be mad if you get us the first class." Bastein smirked, and that only made Avery drop her grin.

Lines of seats were covered in black material: two seats facing front and another two facing behind them. There were also single seats off to the sides, a line dividing them. Both sides had large windows, showing off the scenery.

The three took a seat though Cain sat alone. The train waited for a few minutes before it ignited itself again. The loud engine started, and Cain felt the train pulling him back as it moved forward. Despite its fast speed, he looked out the window when the train pulled onto its scenic route.

Mountains and mountains sat beside each other, stretched out into the distance, nearly covering the entire scenery. Lush swathes of tall green hills appeared into view, sitting below the mountains covered with trees.

They were soon upon a stone bridge with arches that seemed to stretch on forever. Down below the bridge, a sparkling river ran, before darkness took over and Cain realized they were in a tunnel until the light shone back on them again.

With the tunnel out of the way, they then descended down to a flatter train track where once again, they were met with more forests and mountains and a river.

"Ooo! Look at the cute darlings!" Avery squealed.

The animal resembled a deer with brown fur and white spots. The head had the shape of a rabbit with long, floppy ears, but it had the legs of a gazelle. It lifted its head elegantly, but upon catching sight of the train, it then galloped away, out of sight.

As they went away from the river, they came upon a field of grass containing a herd of Wiyans, which took the shape of bison with a bull's head.

"You can see Freyland from here," Cain said, glancing from the window.

"We should go there sometime. Maybe in the summer," Avery suggested, eyeing the small town out in the distance.

Half an hour had passed, and they finally arrived at the designated station. The train slowed down to a crawl before it eventually stopped rolling, letting out steam. The three got up and pushed open the door to get outside. Bastein looked around before he spotted a downward V-shaped building.

"Come on. This way," he said, pushing through the crowds.

The station was quite busy, as the three noticed. People scurried here and there, trying to get to their next destination. More people came in and out of the Bernina Express train while others were walking in.

Bastein pulled the door open and walked into the V-shaped building. The interior was all dark walls with lights attached to the side so people could see where they were going. The three walked down the stairs before they went up another set of stairs and then pushing a door open.

"Warlord Wakeley. Here we are," Cain announced.

The entire village looked as though it had gotten stuck in the past, somewhere in the 80s. The one-hundred-and-twenty-seven acres' park was divided into four areas that seemed to reflect the different eras of the past. From small houses to inns—such as the Ghoul Gawling's, and it was said to be haunted by moans of a ghost from the bathroom. However, there were different theories as to why the ghost moaned, and one of them was particularly absurd. Apparently, the ghost was crying out for much-needed toilet paper—to a passenger train, all of them were scattered throughout the streets.

Most of the buildings were vintage, with shops such as Mrs. Fixit's Uncommon Goods (which carries rare items, special kind of mirrors and more), Flying Funkies (that sells records), or the Hairy Cuts, although the name itself gave it out. Perhaps the most popular shop was the Sweet Corner—located at Tri-City Street—which was packed with parents and children eagerly waiting to get their hands on the sweets.

Bastein pushed through the crowd and a rather large group in the center. It was a tour group.

"...the statue you see in the distance is none other than Warlord Warlo Wakeley. The statue was built in his honor for his heroic deeds by winning the Battle of Wakian..."

Bastein stared at the statue standing on top of the hill, and for a brief second, he shivered uncomfortably. It literally felt like curse statue itself was staring right back at him.

Avery squealed unexpectedly as she hastily went close to Bastein. She looked to the right and saw a winged snake slithering back to its owner. She looked up and saw the bizarre owner who gave her a wicked grin. She stared at the dull blue scales of the snake that had black eyes, but as she was staring at the cold, empty shells, the owner spoke.

"Don't get frightened, Mäitli. They don't attack unless they are provoked..." The owner laughed nastily.

Avery shivered, stepping away from the creature.

They continued to walk straight, and Cain saw a newspaper stand: STANDARD DAILY *for all the best articles you can find!* He then trailed his eyes down to the newspaper stand box where a headline caught his attention.

SOMETHING AMISS IN ESQUIRA

He furrowed his eyebrows, trying to rack his brain for any information he might be able to find, but nothing came up. Was something happening somewhere? This was the second time he had heard of that headline after Avery had mentioned it to Sylvette.

"Look," he muttered, pointing to the newspaper. The two looked at his direction and frowned. "What do you think is really happening here?"

Avery shook her head. "I don't know." But that was strange, though, since it was the second time she was seeing this headline.

Intrigued, Cain walked towards the newspaper stand and took one. The other two followed suit.

"So, what does it say?" Avery asked.

"*The citizens of Esquira are finding themselves a bit unnerved. They believe that they could feel a dark, heavy energy around Esquira and that the energy could belong to Kilhelm. Kilhelm, which is a cursed place known for evil energies and where prisoners would go there to meet their doom, could be awakening once more."*

"Once more? What do they mean, once more?" Bastein asked, eyes wide.

Cain shook his head. "I don't know. *The last time Kilhelm had been awakened was 1,488 years ago, when the world had been met with darkness. The authorities have been investigating the place while also placing extra security. Nevertheless, the Congress of Magia assured citizens that there is nothing to be concerned about."*

"One-thousand-four-hundred-and-eighty-eight years ago...wow..." Bastein replied.

Suddenly feeling uneasy, Cain put the newspaper away into its proper place and walked away.

Wanting to change the topic, Avery turned her head to the side to see a store down the road.

"Let's go to the Oddities Sorceries," she suggested as she saw a gloomy, cobbled dark-brown store that seemed to be separate from the busy streets. "I don't think we have ever been in there before."

Bastein hesitated. "But there's no one in there..." He squirmed.

"You're not scared, are you?" Avery teased.

Chuckling, she dodged the crowd until they were finally at the less busy street. Cain looked up at the street sign labeled Oblivity Road. It seemed to be a perfect fit, he supposed.

The old, barren door creaked as Avery pushed it open, and the moment they stepped in, they definitely didn't feel positive vibes in here. Their happiness suddenly got drained from them, and the entire eerie atmosphere made Bastein feel uncomfortable. He shuffled close to Cain who didn't seem to be fazed by the store's unearthly appearance.

The inside was rather a gloomy and dark place, and stuffy, too. The only light came from the lanterns hanging from the walls. Peculiar objects were displayed all over, from shelves to glass cases.

There was one area Cain found rather unusual. Towards the stairs, there seemed to be a small opening, but it appeared to be closed since there was a black door, shutting off the entrance from curious eyes.

"Is that actual smoke?" Bastein whispered as he looked up at the stairs where the entire floor was covered in thick fog. Cain followed his gaze.

Avery shook her head. "No. It's just a fog. It's...a magical effect just to create the atmosphere to match the eeriness of the store."

"Someone certainly knows their spells."

The three jumped from the unexpected voice, trying to find the source, but they couldn't. However, in front of them, at an old-fashioned till counter, was a shadow.

The silhouetted figure emerged from her spot with her walking cane. The owner had long black hair with rotten flesh, but it didn't appear to be injured. It was as though the woman had tried to conjure a spell, but it had gone wrong, backfiring on her. She wore a torn black cloak over her hunched back.

Avery looked at her nearly skeletal hands, but then, they disappeared under the cloak the witch had used to cover them. She flickered her eyes towards the person and stared at the empty, hollow eyes.

"May I help you?" she asked.

"No, thanks," Cain said almost abruptly. "We can help ourselves."

She nodded. "If you insist."

She then walked back towards her spot, disappearing from sight. It was there Cain was able to see the curtain of beads covering the entrance where the witch came from.

Bastein shivered. "I don't know how you guys can stand this place," he muttered. "Wait! Don't leave me alone!" he hissed as he watched the two going their own ways.

He looked around and saw porcelain dolls displayed on tables, and he got the creepiest feeling he was being watched right now, just from the dolls alone.

He then looked at one particular doll, but something seemed off about it. The head. The head wasn't in the right place—it was turned *sideways*. Freaked out, he scurried towards Avery.

"Wait for me!"

Cain walked towards the closed door that had captured his interest from the start. He stared at the glassy knob shining dully.

"What are you hiding?" he muttered.

He then reached for the knob, but the instant his hand landed on it, a spark of electricity came, shocking him. He hissed and withdrew his touch, rubbing his hand from the tingling feeling sensation.

"Curious, I see."

Cain sighed, knowing the witch was behind him. "What's in there? Why is it protected with enchantments?"

An amusement glint tinkled in the witch's dull eyes.

"Secrets which you might not be able to stand. And as always..." The witch waved her hand around, and it seemed as though she had double the protection. "This door is off-limits to the public," she barked.

"...Hey, Avery? Avery!" Bastein's voice was suddenly loud. Cain whirled around and saw him shaking Avery. "Avery, come on! What's wrong with her?!"

Cain briskly walked to her, the witch following behind. He frowned as he stared at a black box with a ruby stone in the middle. The box had engraved words on it: *Pravum*.

He stared at the ruby stone. When a black mist started to swirl inside, it made him frown. He looked at Avery who seemed to be in a trance, but she directed her hand towards the stone. The mist eventually took the shape of an animal, and there, glinting eyes appeared.

"Watch out," Cain sharply said.

He shoved Avery's hand out of the way and took her spot, hissed when the snake-like animal bit his hand. He withdrew his hand, covering the wound with his other one. The creature then evaporated away, and the stone grew still, as though nothing had ever happened.

"Avery!" Bastein exclaimed as she fell down to the floor, twitching violently. He scrambled towards her, falling down on his knees. "What's happening to her?"

But the witch dismissed it like she knew what was happening. "It's alright. Here..."

The witch walked to her and knelt down. She raised her hand as her cane started to glow and muttered something under her breath. Her hand started to glow a bluish white color. She moved it up and down Avery's body, and eventually, Avery let out a calming sigh as her body went back to normal.

Avery blinked, her eyes no longer wide from shock, then she pushed herself up.

"Easy," the witch muttered.

"Avery...?" Bastein asked, eyes wide.

"I'm...okay..." she mumbled then blinked again. "What happened?"

The witch scowled. "You put yourself in a situation where you know you shouldn't have touched it, *petite peste*. The box showed you what you wanted, but in a way, it deceived you."

Avery scowled at the words *petite peste* but then changed her expression.

"I guess you saved my life. Thanks," she muttered as she pushed herself up. She then looked over to Cain who was mumbling a spell, his hand glowing blue as he went over the injured spot several times.

"What happened?" she asked.

"Nothing."

"That spell you did won't heal you completely. Only a few hours, at most," the witch said. "I could—"

"No. Thank you. I'm fine," Cain interrupted her.

The owner shrugged. "Suit yourself. One dead person I wouldn't mind to lose," she mumbled before she walked away.

This made Cain narrow his eyes.

"Come on. Let's get out of here," he said.

The day ended with the sun going down. The three found themselves back on the Bernina Express, but this time, an uneasy feel stayed with them. Perhaps it was because of what had happened at Oddities Sorceries, but nevertheless, all three of them weren't in a talkative mood.

As the train pulled into the sunset, Avery looked out in the distance. But as she did so, she felt an uncomfortable shiver down her spine despite the warm rays from the sun. She couldn't help but think that somewhere in the distance, somewhere far away, something wasn't right.

And she didn't like it one bit.

CHAPTER THREE

SECRET TREASURES

Avery opened her eyes. She laid in her bed, not getting out but staring at the ceiling, multiple thoughts running in her head. Her mind flashed back to yesterday as she still didn't exactly understand what had happened.

The witch had told her the box had deceived her. She paused, remembering the moment when she'd stared at the box—she'd felt a weird tingling feeling, and for a brief second, it had paralyzed her body. And then...and then...

She'd fallen onto the ground. She also recalled Cain got his hand injured, as well. Did he get deceived by the box, too? She didn't know since he hadn't told her. She sighed. Hard-headed child, as always. Nonetheless, she was glad to be able to live with Bastein and his parents even though they were just friends. Since her grandpa was old, she didn't think she would be able to take care of him by herself, and so Sylvette had been kind enough to offer to have her and her grandpa live at her place.

Avery's eyes turned glassy at the last memory she had of her grandma before she passed away. She missed her so much. She'd never forget her last hug with her grandma.

Deciding she'd had enough of lying on her bed, she pulled herself up and got out of it. The grey floorboards creaked as she walked upon them, and then she resumed her usual morning routine: shower, get dressed, and eat.

Speaking of eating, her stomach growled from hunger, and she put her hand over it.

"Alright, I get it," she muttered.

She then walked out of her room, putting on her cozy sweater and grabbing a fistful of hair to take it out. She stopped and stared ahead.

The house, despite being small, was quite cozy and comfortable, and she didn't mind the smallness. The building itself was an old-fashioned Victorian structure. The inside had beige walls with a chandelier hanging in the entrance of the house. The door was brown, with glass windows. There were also small tables with picture frames, just to make the hallway feel more welcoming.

She then looked to the one bedroom to the side—Bastein's room. There was also an attic, where Cain slept.

The hall was covered by a mahogany carpet that also ran along the stairs. She went down the creaking steps then turned, heading towards the kitchen.

But the moment she reached the kitchen, she stopped. The brown door was closed, and there, in front of the door, were Cain and Bastein.

Smirking, Avery gleefully waltzed towards them and placed a hand on Bastein's shoulder.

Bastein let out a scream, but Cain quickly covered his mouth, muffling it.

"Are you stupid or something?" Cain hissed.

Bastein protested before he glared at Avery, who cackled.

"Go to Hell, Ave!" Bastein replied angrily.

She chuckled before she asked, "So...what are you two doing?"

"None of your business," Bastein snapped.

"There's some kind of a hidden conversation between the parents," Cain said as he ignored Bastein's remark.

"Did you try to ask them if you can join?" Avery asked.

Cain rolled his eyes. "Oh, yes. Totally. I'm sure we'd be in the kitchen instead of outside, eavesdropping," he drawled.

"And besides," Bastein started before Avery could make a remark. "Even if we asked, I'm sure we would get a response, something along the lines of 'Us kids aren't allowed to join an adult conversation.' Or something."

Avery pursed her lips. "Well, that's a pity." Her eyes then sparkled with mischief. "Wait. What if we—"

"Bastein and I already tried it," Cain responded, shutting off her suggestion. "The door's protected with enchantment. Our only hope is to eavesdrop, but so far, I can't really make out what they're saying."

Avery sighed. "Well, that sucks. Wonder what they're talking about."

Bastein shook his head. "I'm sure they will tell us in their own time. So, for now, let's go to the living room and pretend we haven't been here..."

He turned around, ready to get out.

"Too late," Avery said.

The protection wore out, and the door swung open, revealing Bastein's parents and her elderly grandpa.

"Well. I'm sure you three had such *delightful* conversations." The brown-haired, slightly wide woman with a Victorian hairstyle pursed her lips.

"Uh...we talked about our day at the Warlord Wakeley," Avery nervously answered. Unfortunately, that didn't do much for the parents.

"In. *Now*."

Avery winced from the sharpness of the tone, but the three didn't question anything. Not until they were in there and helping out.

The kitchen was medium-sized, with a hard wood floor, forest green cabinets—some of them had glass windows—and brown shelves. Pots hung from a stainless bar above a counter. The stove was turned on, cooking the breakfast for today. The long brown table that sat across the kitchen itself began to fill up with plates and bowls.

Avery let her eyes fall upon a newspaper that was spread out on the brown table. She only had a brief second to look at it—which read:

SOMETHING AMISS IN ESQUIRA—before Sylvette swept it away and gave her a frown.

Bastein looked up at the two who both darted their eyes to his mom, indicating to ask. He looked at his mom before letting out a breath.

"So, um...Mom..." he began. "Was there any particular reason why the door was protected?"

"So kids like you wouldn't barge into a private adult conversation," his mother answered.

Bastein winced.

Deciding it wasn't going to go anywhere with Bastein, Avery took charge.

"Come on," she insisted. "The least you could do is tell us. Like what are we going to do? Go ahead and dig up some fairy tale story or something? Besides, I'm pretty sure it's not real, anyway."

"Come now, Sylvette. Don't be too hard on the kids." The elderly grandpa hobbled with his stick as he walked towards the chair. Avery rushed to him, but he simply dismissed her. "It's alright, darling."

"They shouldn't be a part of it at all," the mom said.

The grandpa sighed, closing his eyes to rest them for a bit before he reopened them. "I really think it's time they know about a historic event. Perhaps even legendary."

"No," Sylvette sharply responded. "They shouldn't. It's nothing but a myth."

"It's only a myth to you because you simply *choose* to *not* believe it, dear," the grandpa said.

"Arvo," Sylvette said.

Arvo, Bastein's dad, simply shrugged. "Once a man's mind is made up, there's no changing it."

Sylvette sighed. "Very well, then."

The grandpa nodded. "Well, then...let's see..."

"Perhaps from the top would be the best place," Arvo responded.

"Yes, yes," the elder muttered. "In the legends, the story starts with magical items. Items that were the key to unlock something more, and said items were forged into one. No one knows where it is or how it's been made. No one but one man. A man named Uris Amos."

"Uris Amos?" Cain asked, puzzled.

"Yes. Uris Amos was a great researcher, and he still remains one of the greatest even today. You see, Uris Amos spent his entire time researching something impossible. He always believed there is something more than what he was led to believe. In his journey, he found something incredible. There was a key—a key to something.

"Now, a key may not seem incredible to most, but to him, it was. It was incredible to him because it could've been the key that leads to another world. He was able to recognize the key for what it was because of the immense power radiating of it the moment he touched it. But of course, he died, and the legend died with him. It is impossible to know what the great researcher had found as it was never recorded in the history itself. Not even in the books." The grandpa sighed. "If you truly want to know what he found, you would have to do it with your own imagination..."

Intrigued, Avery asked, "Did he find anything else? Other than the key..."

"Well—"

"That's enough," Sylvette said abruptly. "The more you tell, the more it will go into the kids' heads, and they will probably continue Amos's work. Who knows what will happen if they actually find the key? It sounds too powerful to be meddling with it."

Avery gave a small glare. "No, we won't. I don't get fairy tales stuck in my head. Maybe these goons, but not me."

"Excuse me?" Bastein raised an eyebrow. "Watch it, Avery. Someday, you'll bite your own words, and you would be a hypocrite."

She rolled her eyes. "As if."

Sylvette fumbled around the stove, grabbing a mitt, and she carried the pot towards the table.

"Alright, then. Breakfast time, and I don't want to hear any more of this nonsense. Especially from you kids."

CHAPTER FOUR

HYPODRIVE

"Do you actually think Uris Amos and this 'key' exists?" Avery asked.

Bastein shrugged. "I don't know, but your grandpa seems pretty set on the legend. He may believe it himself."

"I thought you don't believe in fairy tales," Cain pointed out.

"I was only wondering," Avery snapped. "Besides, what are *your* thoughts?"

"I think it's just baloney. Nothing more than a lost legend to tell kids at night for a bedtime story."

"Oh, yeah? The legend of the Balderdash Unicorn was said to not be real, but then, an explorer actually found one. They were really rare," Bastein said.

"Are you honestly going to believe in some wacko of an explorer? What if he just said that to get more attention? People would do anything to get some these days," Cain pointed out. "Don't believe anything unless you have seen it with your own eyes."

Bastein frowned. "I still say that Balderdash Unicorn are a real thing."

"Alright. Enough of this nonsense. How about we go do something? Like, you know, something upbeat and fun?" Avery grinned.

Cain smirked. "You mean, you want to play Hypodrive? I'm all game, but don't be upset if I win."

"You win? Please. I'm so gonna kick your butt at this. You all know I'm the best," she said gleefully.

"Loser has to do both chores for a month!" Bastein proclaimed as he got a head start, running off towards the field.

"Hey! No fair!" Avery cried out.

They all arrived at the field a bit farther away from the house. The wind blew, making the air breezy. Avery stood across, standing in front of the goal post while Bastein and Cain both stood in front of their own goal post. It was two against one, but that wasn't enough as the rules stated they needed at least *six* players. Sylvette stood to the side, being a supervisor so she could watch the game just in case anything bad happened.

"You all know the rules of the game?" Sylvette called out.

"Yes, ma'am!"

Sylvette stuck her left hand out, palm facing upward, and then she took out her right hand, putting it above her left hand. She swirled her fingers, and a mist of white appeared. The mist swirled around, levitating above her left hand until eventually, a shape was made. It was an oval, with swirls of cloud inside the glass object.

However, the second she made the object appear, more items started to show up in each of the players' hands. Avery looked down and saw a bat-like object that took the form of a leaf. This was what they would use to bat the tear-drop seeds that had just appeared in Sylvette's hands. Sylvette then took the object she'd summoned the first time.

"Remember," she replied, showing the oval shape. "If you catch this gale, your team wins points. You need to have two hundred points in total, so you need at least one-hundred-and-fifty points into the game. You can only follow where the wind currents take you. If the wind gets too strong, I have the right to end this, plus the game can get too dangerous. And it is rather windy today."

Sylvette paused and took a look at all three.

When no one complained or interrupted, she continued and released a breath.

"Alright, then. Everyone, get into your positions. Take your stance, and let me do my magic on you."

She then raised both of her hands and muttered a spell. "Duplicis!"

A yellow streak of magic flew from her fingertips. It moved in a wavy motion, heading towards the three. The spell struck Avery who gave a small gasp before shivering, feeling the magic entering her. Her whole body glowed the yellow color, and there, three copies of the same exact Avery stood beside the real one. The same thing happened to Bastein and Cain, though only two copies were made as Bastein and Cain were already a team.

Sylvette watched as the magic performed itself, and then once it had died down, the color faded away, she conjured up a charm under her breath—"Ventus!"—threw her hands in the air, making them swirl, before she released a white streak that hit the original three and the copies. Once the white swirl had wrapped around the players, it lifted them up, the swirl still around them. Without it, they wouldn't be able to float.

"Players, ready?"

There was a chorus of "Yes!"

Sylvette narrowed her cat-like eyes before she released the command.

"Let the game commence!" she shouted, releasing the Gale.

The Gale orb flew out of her hand and was released into the air, flying freely. One of Avery's players set herself as the goalie while the other three were the players of the game, but each with different objectives. Even though the orb was in the air, the rest of the players, except for the goalies, were busy catching the tear drop balls that were flying through the air. Sometimes, they would spot the orb, but it would be out of reach for them.

The original Avery focused herself, narrowing her eyes as she spotted the ball and grinned. She placed both of her hands at her side, but once she was close to the flying ball, she extended one of them out.

Unfortunately, the closer she got, the wind suddenly picked up the breeze, and it made her widen her eyes, which threw her off-course. However, she managed to stop herself from being completely thrown out of the game.

This made it a bit easier for Cain as he was also closer to the ball. He snatched the required object and then quickly ducked to avoid the copies of Avery before he ascended upwards. He had his attention on Bastein who turned sideways to face him as he happened to be ahead.

"Bastein, catch it!" Cain shouted as he stopped himself in mid-air and threw the medium-sized ball.

The item raced at an incredible speed though one of Avery's copies who was close to grab it, but Bastein grabbed it just in time. He stopped in mid-air for a brief second before he resumed his flying and was heading straight towards the goal post.

"Get it for the goal!" Cain screamed until Bastein was met with a hard tackle that knocked him off-guard, dropping the ball.

"Oof!"

An angry whistle was heard, followed by a shout from Sylvette.

"Avery! Stick to the rules or I'll have you disqualified!" she screamed.

Bastein glared as he rubbed his shoulder from the back while Avery gave him a cheeky smile and blew him a kiss.

"Sorry! I didn't see him there. I think the wind is picking up." Avery grinned widely.

"At least this confirmed everything. You have a breezy mouth!"

"Excuse me!?"

Cain was unaware of the small tackle since he was too busy focusing on the goal, and then, once he was close enough, he narrowed his eyes and grinned wide. He threw the ball as he stopped himself in mid-air once he was a few meters away from the goal post. The sphere rolled through the air, but alas, the goalie made a save by twirling herself around and kicking. This only made Bastein drop his grin.

"I got it!" Cain shouted as he watched the flying sphere coming down. Luckily for him, he grabbed it as his hands made a loud *thud* against the rough surface of the ball. "Woah!" he exclaimed as one of the Avery duplicates zoomed past by him.

Narrowing his eyes, Cain gained his balance back and proceeded to fly towards the goal.

However, he got ambushed when the other copy of Avery came in, zooming from the front. She then smacked the ball away from his grasp, making it fly across the air. Bastein saw the oncoming sphere and was about to grab it, but another duplicate of Avery seized it before he could grab the ball again. With the speed she had, it nearly knocked him off balance.

"Hey! Are you trying to kill us?!" he exclaimed.

Avery shrugged. "I don't control them. They see them as they call them."

Bastein growled but then saw the player was close to the goal. "Bastein, block that! No *not me*! You!"

As the Avery replica came at the goal, she threw the ball. The Bastein replica came after it but failed to block by an inch. The ball went through the post, with Avery's team ending up scoring one hundred and fifty points.

"Yes!" Avery pumped her fist in the air.

The game continued. There were some close calls here and there, and there was one time where Bastein's team scored twice, which put them ahead of Avery. So far, both of the teams were tied. However, as the game proceeded, Avery found out the wind didn't really seem to be going in the direction she wanted it to go.

And it seemed tougher to fight against the wind current, and she also found out she was lacking behind in flying. She glanced to the side to see Sylvette who was constantly watching between the real Bastein and Cain and the fake copies. It seemed she was aware of how dirty both of the teams were playing, making her whistle every now and then and how she was constantly threatening to disqualify them and to end the game.

Since she was busy, Avery smirked, and then she closed her eyes once she was sure her area was safe.

"Celeritas venti," she whispered and gave a small gasp when she felt the cold shiver from the breeze running across her spine.

Her body felt different now; more rapid. Quicker. The wind swirl still around her felt speedier. She knew it wasn't in the rules, for sure, but one thing she didn't know, what she had miscalculated, was the fact that the new wind charm she'd conjured was really *fast*.

She felt the wind current from the front blowing extra strong, and then, as she started to fly forward, it knocked her backwards, hard. She let out a scream as she was spinning around the air and she barely even heard Sylvette's scream.

"Avery! AVERY!"

Sylvette's scream eventually faded away, and Avery felt herself being thrown away, far into the distance, where she landed on the ground with a hard impact right on her face, knocking her out.

CHAPTER FIVE

A LAND WITH CROSSES

Avery gasped as she quickly opened her eyes and let out a raspy, strangled cough as though the wind had been knocked out of her lungs. At first, she had trouble getting some air into her, and she felt like a fish out of water, trying desperately to grab some oxygen. But after getting her breathing into its steady rhythm, she calmed herself down, letting herself heave in and out.

She grunted, giving out a rough gasp. Her eyes were watery, but she dismissed it. She only cared that something was hurting her face. Or at least her cheek. When she brushed the painful cheek, she watched the small pebble tumble back down to the ground. She cringed as she gently rubbed the skin, sure there was a hole there now.

Just her luck.

Grunting, she shakily pushed herself up to her knees while ignoring the small rocks that would stab her at her palm.

"Whew...Okay..." she said to herself, unsteadily. "Well, that was a change of pace for a game, huh? I think I made a big impact this time. It sure was windy." She laughed nervously.

The pale-skinned girl then looked up and found she wasn't in familiar surroundings. She wasn't *home*. She hadn't thought the wind would be *that* strong to knock her away from her home.

Where in the blazes was she? Avery certainly didn't recognize the new environment now surrounding her. In fact, instead of the usual sunny area, this place was drowned in gloom and murkiness. A fog covered a portion of an area in the distance, and it seemed to cover only that part.

Avery gave out a disturbing gasp and shuddered as she saw piles and piles of objects around. She squinted through the darkness only to widen them as she realized what the piles were. Crosses. The hills were stacked with wooden crosses upon crosses, and the loads were scattered everywhere.

Suddenly, she got this sinking feeling she wasn't *supposed to be here* at all. She'd found this place by some sheer dumb luck. But just how *far* did the wind current take her? Where *was* this place? *What* was this place? A place for the dead?

She took one glance around her. No. It didn't look like it was. In fact, this entire place was screaming negative energy, sending off eerie vibes from every inch of it. And she didn't like it one bit. And then...it suddenly felt *cold*. She shivered. This reminded her of Eventide.

What to do? What to do? Regardless, though, she wanted to get out of here, and she wanted help. She wanted warmth. Not the coldness. She wanted her friends. Not loneliness.

Well...maybe she only wanted Bastein, not Cain. Avery found Bastein to be gentle and kind whereas Cain, he was just an annoying, brooding brat. Everything he did seemed to get on her nerves, and he just seemed self-absorbed and always thinking he was better than anyone else. While Cain's parents were working for the Congress of Magia, Avery got stuck with him.

She didn't know how Bastein could deal with him.

She let out an exhale, the misty breath escaping from her mouth. It felt just like winter. She decided she *really* didn't want to stay here and possibly die: she didn't know the area, so she had no idea what lurked around here. But, the location of where she was didn't really help, either. She was just merely surrounded by the heaps of crosses.

So, she began to walk. Regardless, she really hoped Sylvette would come and get her as soon as possible.

In all of her walking, she learned one thing. This whole place felt like a maze with all these twists and turns at every corner, and these crosses certainly didn't help. She came across a pile of crosses where the road split on both sides, but in between them looked to be a broken staircase that led to nowhere. However, in front of the staircase, a few meters high, was an angel statue looming down. But this only made her shudder unpleasantly. Everything about this place was unpleasant. She hated it.

Deciding she didn't want to linger here, she abruptly turned around so she wasn't staring at the angel—or at some kind of monument. Nevertheless, she shook her head and tried to comfort herself that Cain, Bastein, and Sylvette would get her out of here soon.

Hopefully.

Even though many minutes had passed, to her, it felt like an eternity. She had been walking nonstop, and it made her feel exhausted, but still, she hadn't yet found an exit, and she was getting anxious. Worried.

What if they were never able to find her? What if she could never get out of here? What if she was stuck in here *forever*?

Her breath quickened from the panic, and instinctively, she screamed, shooting her hand up in the air, sparks of orange color filling the dreadful sky.

"*Axilium!*"

As soon as she sent the spell—a *SOS* spark—into the air, it died down. She gave a shuddering breath. The cold really didn't help her out, but if she didn't have to use magic too much, then she wouldn't. Not unless it proved really necessary.

However, the sparks weren't the only thing to grab her attention. From where Avery was standing, she suddenly heard a critter noise, almost like a clicking tone. Gasping, she whirled around, staring at the path around her while trying to identify where the noise could possibly come from.

"H-hello?" she stammered.

The sound began to grow louder, but she didn't want to stay here any longer. Avery took off, running to the opposite side, trying to get away as far as possible.

⁓⧸⧸⧸⧸⁓

SHE HAD TO REST. ALL of this walking around, panicking, it was really draining her. She hadn't realized she would be stuck in here for such a long time. She didn't know how many hours had passed—or it was just minutes? She was cold. She was hungry. She was tired. But she forced herself to keep moving. Avery certainly didn't want to die here. Forgotten.

Regardless, she had to keep moving. Whatever she'd heard before, she was certain it was on the move, and she would rather move than get eaten or attacked by whatever that noise came from.

After catching her breath, she resumed walking, grunting, and almost lost her balance but caught it quickly. Time to get a move on.

With a few more minutes of aimless walking, she slowed to a stop. There was something up there, ahead of her, and she couldn't really quite make it out. Maybe it could be shelter. She clung to the hope of this small thought and continued to push herself until she eventually arrived at the place.

It was indeed a building, a temple of some sort, but from what she could tell, it lay in ruins. Parts of the staircase were broken, and there was a medium-sized gap between the stairs and the entrance of the large, brown-yellow temple. The entrance didn't feel welcoming at all with its doors covered in eerie darkness.

Avery climbed up the stairs carefully, and she noticed there were writings carved into the old walls. Words such as *antiqua malum, Hic male dormit,* and forming a nearly broken sentence up on the ledge of the entrance:

Nullum malum, ne male audiam, nec loqui mali

They were all unnerving sentences, but she didn't really have an idea what they meant, only that they all had to do with something about an evil. That was all she could really make out. But after studying the temple, she wasn't so sure if she really wanted to take this place as a shelter: something about it didn't feel right at all.

Cringing, she turned around, and the moment she did, she shrieked as she suddenly found herself faced with a bizarre creature. Not having a second to react, the creature beat her to it and grabbed her ankle and threw her out, away from the temple.

Avery crashed through the pile of wooden crosses, disturbing their rest. She gasped, fumbling her way out, and once she was untangled from the heap, she then took a second to quickly analyze the beast.

The animal had the shape of a spider, but it was large and black and headless. Its terrifyingly long, tall legs made a clicking sound as it menacingly came towards its prey.

Realizing she needed to get away, Avery quickly snapped herself back to reality and scrambled to her feet. What *was* that?

Panicked, she ran away from the beast, but it was surprisingly quick, easily catching up to her. While she ran, her mind began to process information as she was desperately trying to remember the *Book of Creatures: All You Need to Know*. She *knew* it has to be in there. She had read the book once upon a time in Sylvette's study room with her.

The headless spider screeched something awful, which made it hard for Avery to think, and she cringed at the horridness.

She resumed her train of thoughts but then quickly thought of an idea. It might be tricky as she had never done it, but it wouldn't hurt to try.

Eyes narrowed, she made sure there was enough distance between her and the animal. She then slid to a stop, turning around so she was facing the path where the creature had just emerged from the corner. Taking a breath, she raised both of her hands and spoke.

"*Obedio!*" she exclaimed, and from her palms, an unstable golden blast of small waves flowed towards the creature.

The spell struck the beast, which made it shriek, not liking the move its prey was making. It tossed its headless body, trying to get rid of it, but this only made it harder for Avery who was struggling to stand her ground.

Avery growled, realizing just how strong this creature is.

"You obey me!" she shouted.

Alas, the beast simply refused the command. But because of the blast, it walked backwards, ramming itself into a pile of crosses. However, it continued to go on its rampage until it finally broke free and threw a couple of crosses towards Avery who was forced to break the connection.

"*Barrius!*" she said sharply, and a magical shield of a dim yellow color appeared around her, protecting her from the oncoming attack.

The shield died down, but by this point, she was beginning to feel tired. Nevertheless, she didn't let it stop her. There was one more spell she could use—she was pretty sure she could conjure it, but it would take a lot of energy.

Eyes narrowed once more, she flexed her hands before she summoned the spell.

"*Ardenti igne!*" she exclaimed.

She felt something hot burning inside her mouth and begging to be released, and then, a bright fire streak let itself out in a burgundy coil. The attack rushed towards the enemy, and it only pushed the foe back despite its painful screeches.

Avery stood her ground even though the blast was strong, and so, it pushed her back a bit. But she knew the fire spell was almost done. And at last, the fire engulfed the blasted enemy who was screaming something horrid, and she let out a loud, strained gasp as she collapsed to the floor, panting hard. Despite the rough breaths, she gazed at the burning creature thrashing around wildly until all that was left were the smell of burn and bones.

Shaking, Avery lifted her hand up towards her neck and pulled out an hour-glass-shaped pendant. The glass was filled with an amethyst color nearly touching the bottom. She let out another strained gasp and hastily placed the pendant back into its proper spot.

She needed to rest. To be recharged. To be refueled. The three spells had taken a lot out of her, but really, the only ones that had done her more damage were the Fire spell and the Obeying. Avery felt herself growing sleepy, but a small memory snaked its way into her mind while her eyes were starting to close.

A memory that was so distant. So far. So *long ago*.

"Remember, my dark one. It's important to keep checking on your magic life force. You cannot let it be empty."

"What happens if it is empty, Mama?"

The older woman pursed her lips, and an unsettling look etched on her pale face. "You die, dear."

Avery snapped herself wide awake, and this time, she was looking around widely until her eyes returned to normal. She sighed, bowing her head down so her blond hair covered her face.

"Avery!"

She lifted her head back up, blinking. She wasn't sure if she had heard it or if she had imagined it. She laughed shakily, shaking her head and refusing to believe it.

"No way," she muttered to herself. It was probably just the wind.

But there *was* no wind.

"Avery!" the second voice said sharply. More loudly this time.

This time, she widened her eyes as her name finally reached her ears. She was stunned, and she dared to let herself believe *they* were *here*. She stood up and whirled behind her to gaze at the empty path until three figures began to emerge from the shadows. She held her breath, eyes still glued to the scene as though if she had blinked, she would miss it and the figures would vanish.

She allowed herself to let out a cry of relief once she saw the familiar silhouettes. They were here! Bastein, Cain, and Sylvette. Heck, she was even happy to see Cain, for once.

"You guys!" She burst into a full sob, running towards them where she jumped at Bastein, wrapping herself around him for a hug.

Bastein nearly lost his balance, but he regained it and returned the hug.

"You guys found me," she said, a bit hysterically.

"Of course we did. Did you know how many different spells and charms we had to use for the locator spells?" Cain asked.

"Sylvette—" Avery gasped as she pulled herself away from Bastein.

"It's alright, dear," she said soothingly. "We're here."

Cain furrowed his eyebrows and made a nasty expression.

"Ugh. What is that horrid smell?" he asked, pinching his nose so it wouldn't fill his nostrils anymore.

Avery took deep gulps of air before she managed to talk. "There was this creature...a big animal in the shape of a headless spider with long, tall legs. I had to fight it. At first, I thought I could make it obey me, but it was just too strong, and oh! The amount of the evil it had? It was horrible. But since I couldn't use the Obeying charm, I had to use the shield spell and the fire spell...I'm pretty much drained," she ranted.

Sylvette gave her a stunned looked. "Obeying charm and a *Fire spell*? Show me your magic life force," she demanded.

Nervously, Avery pulled her pendant out and winced when a dark look flashed across Sylvette's face.

"We need to get out of here. You need to be refilled on the magic force," Sylvette said.

"I tried to conserve it, but I had to fight an enemy," she trailed off. "Oh! And I also used the SOS spell...I didn't know where I was. I thought I would be stuck in here forever."

Cain rolled his eyes. "Wow. You doubted our ability."

Sylvette shook her head. "Doesn't matter. Let's get out of here. Come, come."

As Sylvette began to leave, the three of them followed her, but Bastein glanced back and gave out a shudder.

"I really don't like this place," he muttered, and the two of them agreed.

"Oh, by the way," Cain said as they were walking. "You're disqualified from the game."

CHAPTER SIX

URIS AMOS

The next morning, Avery couldn't seem to snap herself back to reality. Her mind was entirely focused on whatever area she'd been in the previous day. They hadn't fully navigated the area since Sylvette was able to transport them out.

As the transportation spell had seemed too complicated, Avery hadn't tried to perform it in the first place. Regardless, she was constantly checking on her pendant which was nearly full. The amethyst glow seemed to pulse every time her breath rose up and down as she lay there soundlessly. She wondered if Sylvette had performed a refill energy spell on her while she was sleeping.

But because of this, it also made Bastein unconsciously check his black ring on his middle finger. The oval-shaped ring also had an hourglass carved in the middle, but unlike Avery's, his was filled, all the way to the top. The silver color stood still inside the ring, unmoving.

By the time afternoon arrived, Avery felt recharged. Energized. Her pendant was now full to the top. She, Bastein, and Cain were all sitting at the kitchen table. The occasional sound from the pots that were washing themselves in water could be heard.

"Do you have any idea what that place was yesterday?" Cain asked in a low tone.

Avery shook her head. "No. I would've told you guys if I did, but I don't. It's creepy." She shuddered. She'd have nightmares of that place every night. Something was definitely evil about it. "But it's super evil."

Bastein nodded. "Definitely."

Of all of the places around the world, she would definitely not visit that forsaken place again. Even if her life depended on it. No way. No how. But still, though, she didn't mean to say she wasn't curious about it. Perhaps they could go down to the library and find out. Maybe even Uris Amos...

"Hey, why don't we all go to The Arcane Scroll?" She voiced out her own thoughts. "And you know...while we're at it...we dig up some information about Uris Amos."

Cain narrowed his eyes upon hearing the name. "I thought you didn't believe in fairy tales."

Avery rolled her eyes. "I don't, but aren't you at *least* curious about who he is? I mean, my grandpa did tell us about him, but what if there was more?"

Bastein agreed. "That's not a bad idea. I think we should go to The Arcane Scrolls. Why don't Cain and I search up about Uris Amos, and you can search up about that place from yesterday?"

"Sounds like a plan." Avery nodded.

"Oh, and maybe we can find some more information as to what happened one-thousand-four-hundred-and-eighty-eight years ago. I'm really curious," Cain said.

"Agreed," both Avery and Bastein said.

Later that afternoon, they all went down to The Arcane Scrolls. The library was enormous with its high, rich hard wood ceilings. Almost every ceiling was arched, and there were thousands upon thousands of books all pressed to the tall wooden shelves. Several of the long ladders reached to the top of the bookshelves, and many books were being levitated by the librarians as they were finding the correct spot.

Between the bookshelves was a long room with benches and small black lamps which provided light for the hallway. In the middle of the long room, there seemed to be a staircase that looked like it was going down.

It was slightly packed with people, but the air was quiet. Most of the occupants were reading, sitting at tables, or being helped out by the librarians. They would definitely get lost if one didn't know their way.

The three eventually separated, and Bastein and Cain found themselves at the History section. Bastein was looking through the books while Cain was leaning with his back against the shelves. He crossed his arms over his chest and stared around the area.

"Ugh. There must be thousands of books of Uris Amos in here," he said, annoyed.

"According to the legend from Avery's grandpa, he sounded like a researcher. A philosopher who followed his own beliefs," Bastein said while eyeing the books that could potentially be their lead.

"Wow. That totally made our research even *better*. Congrats, Bastein."

Bastein shot him a look. "Are you going to *help* or are you going to spend your time sulking and shooting sarcastic remarks?"

Cain rolled his eyes. "I'm coming. Don't cry."

Ignoring his remark, Bastein responded. "We got two people here. You go to the other side. See if you have any luck."

"Can't we use a discovery spell in here?"

Bastein shook his head. "Out of every place, the library is the only one where no magic is allowed. No one except the librarians are allowed to use it."

"What's the harm it could do?"

"Gee, I don't know. Burn the whole place down if one spell went wrong?" Bastein offered.

"I don't care," Cain muttered.

"*You don't*. But the library does. And do you know what happens to people who misbehave?" Bastein didn't get a response and so he answered. "It *eats* them." He grinned. "And apparently, there used to be some sort of garden underneath the library for 'medicines.'"

Cain snorted. "That's the stupidest thing I'd ever heard. This library isn't even alive. And medicines? What? They used to sell drugs or something?"

"Something like that."

"If you want to believe in something unrealistic, be my guest. But don't come crying to me if it's not true," Cain said, having no sympathy.

"You're insufferable."

Almost the entire afternoon went by. It was now evening, and most of the people had already gone home. A few people were left, and the two had never left their spot. By now, there were tons of books all piled next to the two boys who were sitting on the floor.

Cain gave up, stating that researching something non-existent was useless, but Bastein refused to give up. They also hadn't seen Avery in a while, but none of the boys seemed to remember about her as they were so busy with their research.

However, Cain did end up finding information about 1488. It was such a brutal period of history to live in, and it made him wish he had never researched it. It was the year where the world met with darkness; a strange, mysterious fog engulfed the entire magical world.

Magic was sacred, revered by the inhabitants. Insians were dying from starvation, from the freezing temperatures that ravaged the world. Many of them perished from magic loss as the evil leader didn't deem them worthy of their witchcraft. Those who survived the purges had magic only because they believed the principles of the wicked head sorcerer.

They, who believed in darkness, were ruled by the arcane arts, fueling their beliefs that the world would be better ruled in the shadows. The followers also alleged that their dark, obscure magic shall be more powerful than those who practiced light sorcery.

Cain shook his head out of his thoughts. Maybe Avery had had more luck.

But it seemed as though Avery had no luck at all. She, too, also had piles of books beside her and was also sitting on the floor. She thought she would look up books about places such as from *Ancient Ruins* to *Legends of the Old,* although there was only one mention—a picture of the place where she had disappeared to, and from there, she was able to go forward, but still no luck.

"I give up," she said, defeated as she eventually joined the two.

Cain nodded. "I don't understand how a library that is five hundred years old has no records of old legends. I thought they would be recorded."

Bastein gave a thoughtful look to the book he was holding.

"How about the Archive Room?" he suggested.

Cain shook his head. "That's only for the librarians, and I don't feel like breaking the rules today."

Bastein sighed. "Then how can we find answers to this puzzle?"

"Your grandpa," Cain said, remembering and looking at Avery. "If he has the knowledge about Uris Amos, then maybe he might have books about him. In his study or somewhere."

Avery bit her lip. "You know, my grandpa doesn't like it when people go into his study without his permission. But I do agree, though. He might have some books about Uris Amos." She paused. "Or, we could just ask him."

"And what? Let him scold us for chasing such a fairy tale even though he's the one who told us about it?" Bastein frowned.

Avery pursed her lips. "Fair enough. I don't need another lecture. We already got it from your mom."

"But are we going to distract him?" Cain asked.

Bastein cringed. "Sleeping spell?" he said tentatively. He immediately changed his answer after seeing Avery's look of disdain. "Or a distraction could work."

"Yeah! Bastein will break your grandpa's favorite vase, and then I'll put the blame on Bastein, and you can sneak into his study!" Cain chipped in. "Man, I hate that vase. Why does he like it so much?"

Bastein glared at him. "Why do *I* have to break it? I don't want him to get angry again."

Cain smirked. "But Bastein, you're good at breaking stuff. Why, I would even say it's your talent!"

Bastein growled. "Wise guy!"

Avery phased them out as the boys bickered, shooting remarks at each other. She still couldn't help but wonder about that place. Just what was it? How come she never saw it until now? Was it meant to be hidden from civilization? She then went back to those words that had been etched into the wall. What did they mean?

"Avery?" Bastein's voice came, but it held concern.

She blinked, shaking her head. "I'm fine."

CHAPTER SEVEN

MYSTERIES OF THE UNKNOWN

November creeped up, indicating that winter was about to begin and the past two months had flown by in a breeze. The weather seemed to have changed overnight. It was a cold, wet grey day in the late afternoon with the wind being brutal, blowing and screeching with all its might. It was getting ready to snow. Esquira could feel it.

The trio found themselves in the warmth of the library, their layers of clothing hanging on the top of their chairs.

"Dimittis. Secreta revelare. Invenio," Avery muttered, and sparks after sparks shot out of her hands, falling down to the books.

Bastein shook his head. "That won't work. I'm pretty sure the librarians put a spell to block spells like those."

The girl sighed. "But where are we going wrong? How can we not find anything on Uris Amos and that place? I refuse to believe we can't find anything."

"Maybe it really is for the history. If it's not meant to be found, then perhaps we should leave it at that," Cain said, putting down the book. "Besides, I'm getting tired. Why don't we continue this tomorrow?"

"Yeah, and maybe proceed with the plan we have." Bastein nodded.

"Okay, okay. That might be for the best," Avery finally agreed.

"SO, HAVE WE GOT IT figured out?" Cain asked, on the lookout.

They nodded.

"Yes, so it shouldn't take too long. I'm sure Grandpa won't mind," Avery said with a wave of her hand.

Cain nodded. "Alright, then. See you in a bit."

Avery gave a small smile before she disappeared to find her grandpa, and sure enough, she found him sitting in a front of a television, watching what looked to be a news channel.

"Hey, Grandpa," Avery said cheerfully.

"Hey, kid, how you doing?"

She shrugged. "Alright." Nonetheless, she decided to go right to the point. "Hey, Grandpa? Um, about those stories..."

"Ah, so you are interested." Her grandpa's eyes glittered.

Avery shrugged again. "Can't help it. It seems fascinating. So...I was wondering if I could go into your study room to look through your books about it? You know I like fairy tales."

He nodded. "Yes, yes, of course you can. I like to say that everyone should read a piece of history. You never know what you would find."

Avery smiled. "Thanks, Grandpa."

AVERY RETURNED TO THE boys with a triumphant smile, and the three went in the direction of her grandpa's study room. They zigzagged through the hallway until they reached a pathway that was slightly enveloped in darkness. They walked down this corridor, and then, the study was there.

The two-glass door was covered with gold frames and doorknobs. It was hard to tell what was inside as it was shrouded in darkness.

"*Inlucesco*," Avery muttered, and a silver light shaped in a ball of a light emitted out of her hand.

She lifted her hand, casting the light across the glass doors. So far, she could see a brown desk and some parts of shelves, and that was about it from what the light had to offer. Sighing, she slightly dimmed the light and studied the doorknob. A small spark glinted out of the peephole, which indicated it was covered with protection.

"*Aperio*." An invisible color wrapped around her hand, but the doorknobs shook and shuddered before it fell back, as though nothing had ever happened.

So, she needed something stronger.

She tried many unlocking spells; each of them stronger than the previous one, until finally, the door decided to open, giving a click and a shudder.

Avery let out a breath, and she placed her hand on the cold knob then pushed it open, placing her other hand on the cool glass. She didn't take her hands off until she'd unlocked the door. However, she lifted her pendant from the shirt and saw she had enough energy for at least two more spells, maybe even three if she was careful with it—her pendant was already half-drained.

"Leave it to your grandpa to have so many protections," Bastein muttered.

"He considers it half the fun," Avery responded.

"*Inlucesco*."

Once more, she was enveloped in the light. Few trinkets were being lit up from the light casting off its dull shine. She could partially see shelves against the walls and filled with books, some neatly stacked and some not. Between the books, in some cases, were items such as an hourglass that twinkled from the light. The sand was almost empty, and it was waiting to be turned over again, to restart.

"Anyone see a light switch?" Cain muttered.

Bastein patted the walls in an attempt to the find light switch until he found it, and he flicked it on. The room instantly flooded with its light, and Avery cancelled her powers.

What am I looking for? Some kind of paper? A journal? Another book?

She glanced at the room. There were more books piled on the desk followed by papers and a fountain pen. Titles read *Legends of the Old, Legends and Myths: All You Need to Know...*and such books were stacked against each other on the surface.

Curious, Avery opened one of them that was all about sacred items and started to skim some of the paragraphs until one caught her eye.

...It is important to note that these sacred items have been lost throughout the history and haven't been found since. No one really knows what they are; some say it could be a key that is said to unlock another world of some sort.

Sighing, she moved away from the books since they weren't being helpful and proceeded to crouch down, feeling the cool drawers against her hand. She tugged on one of them, and naturally, they were locked.

"*Aperio.*"

With an easy click, the drawer gave away, and Avery was able to pull it open. There, in the first drawer, laid a small, black journal. Excited, she gingerly grabbed hold of the journal as though it was so fragile, she was afraid she would break it. She then unwrapped the string around the journal, and with a creak of the old binding, the journal shivered as though it were alive and had been just awakened from its deep slumber.

"Hey, I found a journal!" she called out, and the two boys scurried towards her.

The first few pages were empty, much to her dismay, but as she continued to flip through them, she eventually found something in the journal. Drawings, of some sort. Strange ones.

Avery furrowed her eyebrows as she continued to study them. The symbols seemed to be some kind of a handle...? A key? Followed by an oval...she wasn't sure. It was hard to inspect the drawings since they were so old, fading away of the age.

Bastein tiled his head to the side as an idea came. "Hey, we should take a picture of this. I doubt we're going to remember how the symbols look like."

Avery nodded. "Good idea."

"I'll do it," Cain announced. "*Tortor.*" A bright flash of light came, taking a quick picture of the image.

When there was no more information, Avery placed the journal back into its original spot.

"That was it?" Bastein frowned. "Is there anything more?" he asked, peering down at the drawers.

Avery continued to dig until she met a strange, uneven bump in the second drawer she had opened.

It might not seem much, but she was sure the surface on the inside had a little bit of a bump. Frowning, she started to pat the surface until, sure enough, the surface bounced right back. She started to grab at any loose edges that it might have, but when it was proven futile, she muttered a releasing spell—"*ut seorsum*"—and the parts of the drawer started to disassemble themselves, one by one. She carefully put the pieces on the floor.

To her surprise, there seemed to be a letter of some sort. Curious, she picked it up to examine it, only to frown when she discovered that it was...blank.

She turned over to the other side which was also blank.

Why would my grandpa leave a blank letter?

Cain frowned. "A blank letter?"

Avery shook her head. "I don't know why my grandpa would leave a blank letter."

Cain studied it before he lifted his hand above the paper.

"*Revelare Secretum.*"

A white mist came out of his hand. The mist spread itself on the paper, floating on it for a few seconds before it died down. He let out a sigh of disappointment.

"Nothing," he said after a few minutes of silence.

Avery shook her head. "There has to be something...why would he keep it? Oh, that's right. I also found books, and one of them contains a passage about the sacred items. It wasn't much; it just said that the items were lost throughout the history and hasn't been found since."

"How did the symbols look like again?" Bastein asked, and Avery took out the journal once again since they were here. They could use the image when they weren't here.

"*Projectum*!" A blue-green color appeared in the air, in a form of a hologram.

It was hard to tell, because the journal was so old and the writings and the drawings had been faded over time. Bastein tilted his head to the side to study the faded symbols properly this time. One of them seems to be handle of some sort, but the other one, he wasn't quite sure what to make of it.

"I think this one looks like a key...?" He pointed to the handle. "But I can't be sure. The images are impossible to tell."

Avery sighed. "Well, at least we got something."

Cain frowned. "I think the 'key' looks more like a cross. I don't know; those weird stick things that are poking at the side resembles more of a cross."

"Maybe," Bastein agreed. "But...let's leave this mystery for now..." As if on cue, his stomach growled. "I'm hungry."

Cain rolled his eyes.

"You're always hungry," he muttered and handed the paper back to Avery who took it, putting it in her pocket.

She was feeling quite drained, so she decided sleep would be best. "You guys go ahead. Unlike you, I had to use most of my magic, and it's making me tired."

The two went their way, and Avery eventually reached her bed and fell asleep.

CHAPTER EIGHT

CHRISTMAS

Avery flickered her eyes until she opened them fully. She stared at the blank wall in front of her until she rolled to the other side. It was comfy and warm here, and she didn't feel like crawling out of bed. Besides, the air was cold, which further prevented her from getting up from her cozy bed.

As she was snuggling, her gaze rested down upon her pants hanging over her dresser. The letter which she had found in her grandpa's study room was lingering there as though waiting for her to unveil its secrets.

She groaned, nuzzling her face deeper into the pillow. Was she really that tempted to find out? Sighing, she finally gave up after a few minutes and dismantled herself from bed sheets. Still in her PJs, she walked with bare feet on the wooden floor and took the letter out from the back pocket of her pants.

She gasped, eyes widening at the sudden reveal. It must've happened overnight.

There, the letters were slowly appearing. She hadn't gotten much deciphering done, therefore, she decided to wait until the paper was complete. She shivered then glanced at her blinds, walking towards them to peek through.

She let out a small gasp of delight. White, glittering crystalline powder rested upon the roads, covering them and the sidewalks like a soft cushion. The entire area was doused like a winter wonderland, so magical and sparkling, settling in the silence.

It's Christmas!

Oh, heavens above! Christmas was here—

"AVERY! IT'S CHRISTMAS! AVERY, GET DOWN HERE!"

Christ above, he *always* had to be the loud one on *every* Christmas day.

"Really, Bastein," she muttered.

Avery pulled on a mahogany sweater and went down the stairs as soon as she opened her door. She gasped at what she saw. The entire house was covered with decorations, and it was magical to see how everything was decorating itself. She touched the garlands wrapped around the stair rail, and upon reaching the last step, she noticed how the enchanted snowflakes were falling from the ceiling to create an illusion as though they were real.

She watched, delighted, as three white unlit candles floated until they reached the table, placing themselves there before lighting up with fire, creating a heavenly glow. Even the walls were covered with enchanted frost, which made her shiver from the cold.

The entire house was filled with Christmas magic, all joyful and merrily enough to lift anyone's mood. Garlands upon garlands were scattered throughout, each of them hung against the wall. Stockings were hanging at the ledge of fireplace. A big wreath had also been placed upon the wall, hanging above the fireplace.

A large, decorative Christmas tree stood proud, huge stacks of Christmas presents laid beneath it, beside the ivory couch. Its ornaments were busily floating in the air as if they were finding a spot to be included into the warmth of the branches. The tree was adorned with apples, bells, snowflakes, and sugar cookies, all of them in the shape of something festive. The glow from the candles of the tree cast a warm radiance around the entire place. The whole room was filled with Christmas decorations from colorful baubles on the tree to tinsel to garlands to sparkling lights.

An angel was standing atop, giving off its brilliant warm and powerful light. Avery wrinkled her nose, catching the scent of something so delicious: a mixture of cinnamon with a hint of ginger followed by chocolate. Gleefully, she waltzed into the kitchen which was busy with making all sorts of delicious treats. The turkey was sitting on top of the oven, steaming and juicy, glistening with the gravy, which made her mouth water.

She groaned from the scrumptious smell of food. The shiny, juicy ham was carefully sliced into perfect slices lined up just right, and it was surrounded by scalloped potatoes with melted cheese. The melted cheese gleamed deliciously with pieces of bread around it. Some side dish such as red cabbage and chestnut stuffing also accompanied it all.

But she knew this would all be for later, for dinner.

She could smell the honey of the scrumptious cookies sitting innocently on the plate, stacked neatly.

Basler Läckerli.

She groaned. She *had* to have one of them...those were her favorite cookies of all—filled with honey, almonds, and candied peel, completed with Kirsch.

She had to eat one...

"Ah, ha! Hands off!"

A smack came on her hand, and Avery yelped, withdrawing her hand.

"That hurt!" she whined, massaging her fingers.

Sylvette grinned. "You have to wait, darling dear. You just got up, and this is all for dinner."

Avery groaned. "But the cookies..."

Sylvette smirked. "Nope."

She sighed, knowing she had been defeated. "Fine. I'll just suffer with Bastein and Cain."

"So dramatic."

Sulking, she walked away from the kitchen, hoping to find the two boys.

"Bastein!" she called out, searching the place.

"In the hallways!"

Grinning, she followed his voice until she reached the hallways where she saw him hanging up some lights against the wall, illuminating the path. Cain was completely covered with enchanted snowflakes which he had conjured while putting more frost upon the walls.

"Did you see the kitchen?" she asked eagerly.

"Yes! Can't wait to dive in. There are all sorts of food. Turkey, ham, scalloped potatoes, red cabbage…"

"Basler Läckerli," she supplied.

"And Baumstriezel, Chestnuts, Christstollen…"

"You guys are not helping," Cain muttered.

"And to top it off, the fondue!" Avery grinned.

Bastein grinned. "Don't let go of your fondue!"

"Oh, I won't, *darling*." She smirked.

"But that is all for dinner…" Bastein sighed.

"Yeah…" she sighed, too.

"But, in the meantime, let's finish the decorations!" Bastein said.

DINNER EVENTUALLY CAME, and the three scurried towards the kitchen. It had taken the whole morning and the afternoon to decorate the house. A few minutes later, everyone had joined the table to eat, and the whole atmosphere was filled with Christmas joy.

Grinning, Avery saw the fondue, and she excitedly grabbed a piece of bread and dipped it in the hot, melted cheese. However, as she was about to raise it up, she squeaked when the bread slipped out of her grasp.

"Ah, ha!" Bastein exclaimed in triumph. "You have to kiss Cain!" he cackled.

Cain sneered. "I'd rather get infected with poison."

Which, speaking of poison, Cain glared at his injured hand from when they had been at the store at Warlord Wakeley. Sure, it was slowly healing since Sylvette was giving him medicine that would heal it, but it was still there.

"Touché," Avery drawled.

"Kiss, kiss!"

"No," Cain groaned.

"Grandpa." Avery helplessly looked at him, but her grandpa's eyes twinkled with mischief.

"Sorry, dear, but it's the tradition."

She cringed. Taking in a deep breath, she leaned forward and quickly pecked Cain on the cheek before hurriedly withdrawing away from his touch.

"Gross, gross," she muttered, glaring at the fondue.

THE TOWN CENTER OF Rue Blanche was incredibly busy and quite a fascinating sight to behold. Multiple lights twinkled in the evening from the stalls adorned by the Christmas lights. Music was playing in the background from the show event. A merry-go-round dazzled the crowd with its own display of spectacular lights. A gigantic tree perhaps stole the show with its brilliant display of lights and the fancy ornaments decorated with red and gold color.

Enchanted stars and icicles were hanging up at the ledge of the stalls' roof. Charmed snowflakes were falling as the kids released the spell from the jar, testing out the newest spell—which enabled the spell caster to turn into a snowman—that had hit the vendor.

"Look, I'm a snowman!" a kid exclaimed with a muffled voice.

He indeed looked like a snowman as his whole body was enveloped by large snowballs. The whole shop was filled with magical potions and spells that allowed the customers to test them out. Some customers, particularly kids, appeared like a gingerbread man! There were even new spells that smelled of gingerbread and cocoa and hot chocolate.

"Fairy floss for you, *mademoiselle*?" a seller asked.

Avery's eyes went wide with delight as she saw the mixture of blue and pink cloud of sweet, whipped-up with sugar gathered around the stick.

"Oh, thank you!" She accepted it and gave a tip.

The man bowed with the tip of his hat. "A thank you from me."

Avery savored the sweet caramelized sugar that dissolved in her mouth, the taste of berry left behind. She loved fairy floss.

The market was extremely busy, and she tried her best not to get swallowed up by the huge crowds. She could hear music and chatter and laughter filling up the air. She loved Christmas markets. She grinned at the small bag she was carrying, filled with cute, decorative ornaments such as a fairy, an angel, and snowflakes.

She spotted Bastein and Cain who were huddling up by the great fire pit, trying to warm themselves up. Huh, she thought, it wasn't that cold. She walked towards them, and Cain noticed she was eating the fairy floss.

"I see you haven't missed out on the food."

"As if I would. The food at Christmas markets is the best stuff," she replied. "Have you guys found anything you liked?"

"Not particularly. Can we go home? It's cold," Bastein whined.

Avery shrugged. "I suppose. I think I'm done."

The three started to push their way out of the crowd until the loud noise faded into the background and they were back on the street, away from the lake where the market was held.

Cain glanced back at the crowd that now looked like twinkling balls from all the lights displayed and peered at Avery a few meters away from him. Sniggering, he scooped the snow, forming it into a snowball, and threw it at her in the back.

Avery gasped from the sudden impact, and she nearly dropped her bag while Bastein looked at her with surprise. She whirled around and glared at Cain who looked suspiciously calm.

"What was that for?" she snapped, marching towards him.

"What?" he asked innocently.

"Why'd you throw a snowball at me?"

"Relax. It's only a snowball."

"Whatever."

Avery stormed off into the streets with Bastein hanging back, a curious look on his face.

"Avery doesn't explode like that." He frowned. "She would laugh it off and get you back."

Cain narrowed his eyes, staring at the distance where Avery stalked off. "I think something's up with her."

CHAPTER NINE

SOMEONE'S HURT

Avery muttered a curse as she entered her room, closing the door. She took off her jacket and threw it on her bed. What was the reason Cain threw the snowball? Did he think it was funny? She sighed. Perhaps she was overreacting, but still. She didn't appreciate immature pranks such as that one.

Regardless, she turned to her drawer and opened it, only to reveal the letter she had been waiting to check again. She let out a small gasp, eyes wide as she grabbed the letter from its spot.

There, on the paper, symbols like what she had seen on her grandpa's journal were etched. But this time, it looked as though it was complete. A few days had passed, and it seemed as though the letter had had some time to be fully revealed. She walked to her bed and sat on it, studying the paper.

Maybe Cain was right. It did look more like a cross instead of a handle. But what was the other symbol? An oval? A circle? She wasn't sure, but she stared at it as though doing so would give her answers. What could these mean? She wasn't sure if she should go back to her grandpa's study room to look for more clues—she could be discovered the second time around.

Sighing miserably, she withdrew her gaze from the paper and stared at her mirror hanging up on the wall. After gazing at it for a few minutes, a small realization dawned upon her as she studied her own reflection. She looked back down at the other symbol, and she lifted the paper so that it covered the mirror.

Huh. Interesting.

The letter laid right in front of the mirror, so that it matched the position of the oval symbol. It nearly resembled the same shape.

She bit her lip before withdrawing. It didn't seem like her idea was going anywhere. But, for now, she would see the symbol as an oval. She paused to think about the shapes.

Bastein's father did have a sense of unique stuff when it came to collecting old items, and they were typically held in the basement away from Sylvette's eyes since she thought those items were garbage and useless.

That being said, perhaps Avery should start at the basement in hopes to find oddities for this search.

AVERY TURNED ON THE light bulb. The dimly-lit basement was old, with wooden floors complete with wooden shelves filled with antique, bizarre items. There were strange vases that held faces, or certain sculptures that seemed to have a large head with three hands on each side—hands hovering above the head. It was quite abnormal to see some of the stuff Arvo had been collecting over the years.

She shrank back when she saw a necklace with skeleton bones as its base followed by a skull attached to the bones. This reminded her of when she'd been at that witch's place...

She wasn't sure if she could be a witch. Sure, they could have a little more power than Insians, aka what she was. Insians had magical ability where their magic could be used based on their life force. Every Insian was like this; they all had magical objects.

However, it was possible to add more magic to their life force limit. To do that, they had to go to the Congress of Magia where they'd present their case as to why they needed more magic.

Very few Insians had been approved for such cases; these would mostly go to Insians who would do heavy duty such as building houses and things requiring more magic. Or taming dangerous creatures as that would demand more effort and energy since some Insians were tamers for such creatures and would put on a show.

However, getting an increase to their magic limit might take a few months or even a year, depending on the situation. Regardless, it was important for Avery to check on her pendant every time she used her magic; she couldn't let it be drained.

Shivering, she continued to look at the shelves, passing by one with a sculpture where the head had a mouth opened so wide, it felt like it would swallow her up. The palms were placed on the floor as though they were getting ready to walk any moment.

Heavens above, she mused. Why *did* Arvo find these objects so fascinating?

She knelt down when she spotted a small, medium-sized cabinet with glass doors. She pulled the door open to find stacks of old books placed against each other, untidy and unorganized. She coughed as she pulled out the books, dust coming out of its spot. It would be nice if these could be cleaned once in a while, but hardly anyone came down here. No one was interested in these as much as Arvo was.

Avery brushed off the dust on the books, revealing titles such as *Lost Worlds, Ancient Languages and their Disappearances, Uncovering the Ancient Languages,* and more. Biting her lip, she resumed her hunting until she let out a small gasp when landing on a book titled *Symbols of the Old.*

Eagerly, she withdrew the book and started to skim its pages, but then stopped once she found a passage that seemed to be talking about what she was looking for. At least, she hoped.

It has been stated quite a few times that certain sacred relics had been lost throughout history. However, it should be noted that such relics did exist at one point in time, and they had befallen on a man named Uris Amos. It is said that these relics were to be created into a key, but the function of the key is unknown.

Avery sighed. But where was the key? And how was it related to the symbols she'd found in that letter?

⸻ ✕✕╲╲✕✕ ⸻

"HAS ANYONE SEEN AVERY?" Cain muttered.

They were all sitting in the living room, Avery's grandpa watching TV while Sylvette and Arvo were stirring hot chocolate.

"No. Have you checked her room?" Bastein asked.

"No, I guess not," Cain muttered.

He turned around and walked towards her room, even though he wasn't sure if that's where she'd be. But, considering he hadn't seen her since they had left the market, maybe she would be in there. It had been a day since their trip there.

He stood still when he reached her room, but then suddenly stopped and regretted his choices.

Must he? He supposed he had been mean by throwing a snowball, but he hadn't meant any harm with it. Also, he hadn't expected Avery to lose her cool like that. Usually, she just brushed it off. Strange.

Knock, knock.

"Hey, Avery?" he called out.

He waited for a few minutes until he got fed up, stuffed his hands in his pockets, and started to walk away, but his subconscious mind stopped him. Maybe she was sleeping. He turned to look back at the door, staring at it before he finally gave up and knocked again.

After a few minutes of waiting, he spoke again.

"Avery, I'm coming in. Please don't kill me. I just wanted to say that I'm sorry," he started as he opened the door. Much to his surprise, the room was empty. "Avery?"

He cautiously walked into her dimly lit room, looking around in case she was maybe hiding or something. He didn't know. But then, his eyes fell upon a piece of paper on the bed. Curious, he walked towards it only to gasp, eyes wide. It was the paper which Avery had found, but something was written on it.

He hadn't thought his revealing spell would have worked on it...but there it was. Symbols were written on the paper...but...

Didn't Avery say she found nothing other than the paragraphs from the books? Angry, he let the letter fall to the floor and stormed out of the room.

CHAPTER TEN

ONCE WRITTEN AND NEVER SPOKEN

Bastein eyed Cain with a cautious look upon his return to the living room. He could feel that something was off about him, but he wasn't sure as to what it was.

"Did you find her?" he asked.

"Maybe...maybe not," Cain snapped, which made Bastein jump and startle.

"Alright, don't need to bite my head off," he muttered.

Annoyed, Cain glared at him. "Can you get up? We have to clean our rooms, remember?"

Before Bastein could reply, he yelped when Cain dragged him up and pushed him forward so they were walking towards the hallway, away from the parents.

"What?"

"She lied," Cain said, getting straight to the point though Bastein furrowed his eyebrows in confusion.

"Who lied? About what?"

"Avery. Remember how we had that paper where nothing was shown? And I did that revealing spell?"

Bastein nodded.

"Well, guess what. Some strange symbols actually *appeared* on that paper, and our dear friend 'forgot' to tell us about it."

Bastein frowned. "Why would she not tell us? We're on this quest as much as she is."

"*That's* what I would like to know."

"You think she did it on purpose?" Bastein asked.

Cain shrugged. "I don't know, but I think it's time we talk to her."

AVERY RUBBED HER EYES from exhaustion. She had been going on for too many hours, and her brain was exhausted and getting ready to shut down from all the research she had done so far.

She closed the book and placed it back in its proper spot. She wouldn't think this research was a failure, but it wasn't really a success, either, though she wished the books elaborated more on those relics instead of saying the typical stuff: "they have been lost throughout history."

Regardless, she still did have more to go on, but not today—she desperately needed a break and water. She was getting a headache from all the reading while being dehydrated.

She stretched her legs from her cramped sitting, extending her hands and legs, and yawned. Groaning, she got up and massaged her sore back before she moved herself to the side to relieve her posture. That stretch was much needed.

After cleaning up the mess, she decided to go upstairs and maybe hang out with the boys and possibly...apologize to Cain. She hadn't meant to snap at him. It had just been a harmless throw, and he hadn't meant any harm. She didn't know why she'd reacted that way, though. Usually, she would just shrug it off and be on her way.

Weird.

As she got out of the basement and turned to the left, she heard voices that sounded like the boys. Smiling, she went towards the voices only to stop when she heard her name.

"...why would Avery lie to us? We're on this quest as much as she is." That was Bastein.

"I don't know." Cain.

"But she said there was nothing on the paper when you tried out that revealing spell..."

Avery tensed. How did they know...? She hadn't told anyone. In all honesty, she had meant to tell them, but she'd been waiting for the paper to be completed.

"I don't know, but I think we should talk to her."

She closed her eyes, released a breath, and walked out of her spot while pretending she hadn't heard anything.

"Hi, guys!" she chirped.

Cain twirled around only to glare at her, which made her wince, and she bit her lip.

"What's going on?" she asked, cautiously. "You guys aren't usually this tense, not since Bastein accidentally drank what he thought was carbonated tonic though it was just spiders' blood in the end."

Bastein cringed. "*Don't* remind me. That was a nightmare."

"You wanna know what's going on? I *think* you 'accidentally' forgot to tell us something important," Cain said, immediately jumping to what the problem was.

Avery tensed. "Like what?"

"Why don't we go to your room? For privacy?"

Gulping, she followed the two into her room, and once in there, Cain bent down to pick up the paper that had fallen to the ground when he left.

"Care to explain?" He showed the paper that contained symbols. "You said nothing was shown."

Avery frowned. "Which was the truth, but after we came back, the symbols started to appear."

"Why didn't you tell us?" Bastein asked.

She bit her lip. "I really did want to tell you guys, but it actually took a while for the letters to appear. I think it's completed now."

"Really?" Cain raised an eyebrow. "Have you found anything during your disappearance? We were looking for you."

She nodded slowly. "Yes...I was in the basement, searching through Arvo's stuff—"

"You *went* through my dad's things?" Bastein demanded. "Avery—"

"Can I finish?" Not waiting for his response, she continued. "So, we didn't identify the symbol correctly. However, the sacred relics are said to be lost through history. Regardless, they say that it *did* exist at one point in time, and it was held by a man named Uris Amos. It was also said that these relics were used to create a key, but the function of the key is unknown. And that is all I found from a book."

Bastein frowned. "A key?"

"Look, you guys. More symbols..." Cain announced, holding the paper so everyone could see.

Helpless, Avery shook her head. "What could they mean?"

Bastein stared at the symbols as though that would help give him ideas until an actual idea popped inside his head.

"Hey, I know! We could go down to the Eventide to find out more..."

Cain widened his eyes. "You want go to down to where the dark lives? I'm usually not afraid of this stuff, but I heard they sacrifice people down there, and they make a cult. And, they drain people's magic. You're mad."

Avery rolled her eyes. "You believe too many things. It'll be fine, and I think it's a great idea. What place would have more forbidden stories than Eventide itself?"

"IT'S RIGHT AROUND THIS corner," Avery announced as they went down another set of unsettling stairs underneath a tunnel.

"And this is how we get murdered," Cain said cheerfully.

"Shush," she replied.

They arrived at an empty spot where nothing was in front of them except for the stairs they had just disembarked from as well as the arch.

After studying the arch opening in front of them, Avery lifted her hand so that it hovered above her other one.

"*Ad scalpere,*" she muttered, and as quick as lighting, a blade of light was summoned.

It quickly sliced her hand, which made her wince a little, and then, she lifted her bloody palm and waited. After a few minutes, the rocks started to shift left and right, some crumbling down due to the shifting until it eventually created an entrance.

"Well, let's go!" she replied joyfully, muttering a quick healing spell, and the three entered, all of them casting a light spell.

True to its name, Eventide was dark and gloomy and narrow. And it didn't help that Eventide was underground, making the air stuffy and unclean. Even though it was under the ground, it didn't seem like it since it looked like it was a place of its own. The small buildings seemed to be tight against each other, pressing into one another as though they were trying to make more room. There were tents scattered throughout the place where people dressed in otherworldly outfits were trying to sell their forbidden items.

If the items weren't creepy enough, it was perhaps the clothes that also made Cain cringe just by looking at them, and he was sure he would be traumatized by the time they'd finished their business here. Clothes that seemed to be webs covered many of their bodies with dark decors such as dark flowers and bats that seemed to *move* and didn't look friendly.

Other people wore what resembled wood, but Cain wasn't sure if it was real wood they were wearing. Bones also seemed to be worn as clothes the farther down they went.

"Can we *please hurry up* in here?" he muttered, stiffening.

"Relax. Nothing will happen," Avery mumbled.

"Is that blood on that person?!" he hissed.

Bastein's stomach lurched as he saw a woman with gritty, uneven teeth smiling at them. There was a bone necklace around her neck, her hair tied in a high, tight bun, but her long red dress really did seem like she wore blood, and it might even be. However, there was something off about her pale features, and that was her eye. It seemed to be missing since there was a black hole where the eye should've been, spiders and creepy crawlers slithering out of the hole.

"Avery," Bastein moaned.

She shrugged. "Your idea."

The three of them continued to move forward while Cain and Bastein were desperately trying not to look at the people. One of them even had a skull for head while the rest of the body seemed human, but Cain didn't want to stay to find out.

Regardless, it did unnerve Avery just a little bit, but she found the whole market quite fascinating, and how having the light on was their only savior. They needed the light, otherwise, the entire place would be submerged in darkness, and they wouldn't be able to see. Without it...who knows what could happen? Would they become as the citizens of Eventide without the light? Soulless and trapped while their own body slowly started decaying?

They eventually arrived at their destination. The store seemed small and dark, with a dull light illuminating the inside. The old wooden board across the store had something written on that said: *Vetiti Cartis et Scientia* with the letters fading.

Avery pushed the door, and the scent of old books wafted onto them from the interior. The store was filled with books stacked all over the room. There seemed to be a spiral staircase in the middle that appeared to go nowhere, stretching to the ceiling.

Ahead of the trio, there looked to be a medium-sized arch window also filled with books.

"Wow...someone's really invested," Cain muttered as he hopped over a pile of books on the floor.

"Is there anyone here?" Bastein asked, looking around the wooden store.

"The name's Draugur. How may I help you?" a silky, low voice asked.

The trio jumped as a mysterious figure appeared from the staircase, descending down. The man didn't seem to be tall and had stilted, glassy grey eyes with wide cheekbones, a narrow forehead, and a narrow chin, his face defined in a diamond shape. His shoulder-length platinum hair exposed the rim of his ears that were folded forward slightly, which gave an appearance of a cup. He wore elegant black clothes.

"We're looking for some knowledge about these symbols," Avery answered as she fished out the paper from her pocket.

The man took the paper and studied it for a minute or so before he handed it back.

"The ancient language is what you seek," he mused aloud and lifted his hand in the air, muttering a spell.

Soon enough, the books started to fly around the air as though he were searching for a specific book. In that split second, Bastein saw his hand that was wrapped in gauze, and he wore a ring with an amethyst stone. Upon his gaze, the man allowed his sleeve to fall so that it covered his injured hand. He gave a look at Bastein who held a stony expression before giving the book to Avery.

"This will be the book you need. The symbols you have is an ancient language called Enoia. You'll find it here."

"Thank you," Avery muttered as she started to get the book, but the owner quickly snatched it back and gave a thin smile. Avery narrowed her eyes.

"Not so fast, though. With a book as valuable as this, it requires a price."

Avery stiffened. "Name your price."

He chuckled before he stretched his hand out, grabbing Avery who widened her eyes. Cain and Bastein were ready to fight him if needed, but Cain noticed that the owner merely whispered something in Avery's ear.

He then pulled back with a discomforting smile. The owner gave a curt nod before he disappeared in the shadows.

"What did he say?" Cain asked.

"Nothing," Avery said abruptly.

"Did you see his hand?" Bastein hissed once he was gone.

Cain shook his head. "No."

"It was all injured. I wonder what happened," he ventured aloud before Avery spoke, interrupting their thoughts.

"Look. It's here." She gasped. "*Enoia* is an ancient language that has been lost throughout history. Not much us known about this language, but one can say that this has been used as a form of communication to converse with otherworldly beings."

"Otherworldly beings?" Bastein echoed. "As in...? What? Mystical creatures? That kind of sort?"

Avery shrugged. "I'm guessing, but it doesn't say much about these symbols. It only illustrates what they look like."

"So...you guys think that the key—if we find it—it'll open some world?" Cain asked, making the connection.

Avery closed the book with one hand, causing a slam that made Bastein jump. "That is possible. But who knows?"

Bastein looked around. "Can we take that book home, by any chance? I'm sure it'll be useful, and besides, he just gave it to us."

Avery glanced at the door and mused. "Would it be so easy?"

She played around with the thought by walking towards the door, and the minute she pushed the panel open, she gasped softly as the book gave her a small zap and it flew towards the counter before landing on top of it.

"Never mind," Bastein muttered.

CHAPTER ELEVEN

HIDDEN MESSAGES

Cain stared at the symbols, his face furrowed in concentration, but then sighed. They had just gotten back from Eventide—and thank God they did. He hadn't thought he'd be able to spend another second in that world. Still, though, the way the owner's hand was injured...was it possible he'd tried to do something with his magic and it had overloaded, which had ended in him injuring his hand?

Cain shook his head. He wasn't sure. Speaking about the owner, he was still wondering what kind of a price deal he had made with Avery. Every time he asked her, he would always receive the same answer, which was: "Nothing." As she said.

He supposed he had to drop it since he would never get the proper answer he wanted. However, he must admit they'd made slow but good progress, though he wished he'd found more information about these symbols.

"We need a guide for this one. Anyone have any idea?" Bastein asked, but the two shook their heads.

"We can't ask your parents and your grandpa. They're going to refuse, and we told them we wouldn't pursue this," Cain insisted.

Bastein sighed. "Then, what do we do? We don't know these symbols. And to be honest, that book we had from Eventide wasn't really helpful."

"Yes, but we now know what the language is called," Avery pointed out.

She stared at the letter, deep in thought though what Bastein had said had triggered something in her. She was sure Sylvette would have some books on these ancient languages.

Sylvette only had books like these because she was interested in studying them, and she used to be a historical linguist. Every time Avery had asked her why she had old books, Sylvette would reply by saying she was fascinated by them and thought it was a good idea to remember them. She would say they could learn something from them.

Avery shook her head. "I'm pretty sure your mom would have books on these. That's why we need to go into her study room for more information. I'll just ask her if I can go into her study room."

Bastein groaned. "And what will you give her as an answer? Remember what happened last time?"

Avery mused on the thought. She did remember what happened, and that's why she no longer had access to the study. She'd been a child back then, an inexperienced Insian, too. She'd seen a book about spells and had decided to use one. Of course, because she'd been inexperienced, the spell had gone badly, and Sylvette hadn't been there at the time. Upon hearing the explosion, Sylvette had rushed into her study to find Avery in soot and the place a mess.

However, time had passed since the incident, and Avery had grown more mature with her magic. But still, Sylvette refused to give her access to her study room in case the same thing happened again or if Avery's magic got out of control.

"Wait...so going to Eventide was useless?" Cain asked.

Avery shook her head. "I wouldn't say it was useless only because we now know what the language is called and researching it would be easier...I think. But anyway...do we agree on this?"

Cain said "yes" at the same time Bastein said "no," but Avery pretended not to hear him.

Bastein smirked. "I hope you're ready. Her study isn't easy to get in."

AVERY GROWLED AS A burn hissed onto her flesh, and she quickly withdrew her hand from the scorching heat. She had figured there would be enchantments to keep nosy people out, but *why* did it have to be a burning spell as one of the enchantments?

"*Rejuviltus*," she muttered as she waved her hand over the burn, and a smooth, golden flash appeared. After a few seconds, her hand looked as though the burn had never been there.

She racked her brain for a spell that would be able to melt this burning charm, but it would have to be stronger than this one. She turned to the two for ideas.

"Anyone know a charm stronger than this?"

"We could do a melting charm that would be twice as strong as this one. You know, the *sciogliere*."

She nodded. "We could try that one." She stepped back, cleared her throat, and said the charm. "*Sciogliere*."

She pointed her finger at the lock where a streak of orange spark flew out in a blur and struck the lock, which melted. The heavy lock shuddered before it fell down to the floor with a *clang*.

Avery let out a sigh. One down, and probably three more to go. She looked down at the lock. They would need to find a way to cover that up.

"Now what?" Cain asked.

Avery walked up to the door to test out the handles which proved to be locked; nothing to it. She muttered a spell—"*Apero*"—that enabled one to unlock the handles, and it did so. But after the locked handles, Bastein couldn't help but grin at the next set of enchantments.

"Huh, that was easy," Avery replied, cautiously.

She then pressed down the handle and opened the door, and she stared at the open entrance with a skeptical look. But she decided it was okay to go in since she couldn't find anything wrong with the picture, and then she decided to walk to the opening until...

THUD

"Ow, for the—" she started to swear, but Cain quickly shushed her as she held her nose. Bastein laughed.

Cain glared. "Instead of being a jerk, how about you help?'

Unexpectedly, Avery's eyes started to widen, and she was about to scream until Cain clasped his hands over her mouth so as to not give out their location. She muffled her voice desperately as she thrashed around, trying to get out of Cain's grip.

"Bastein!" Cain growled.

"Okay...okay..." Bastein muffled a laugh as he went towards the door and muttered a *dissolvere*, a spell to make a magical barrier disappear. But he frowned since the barrier was still there after his finger touched the force field. The barrier created a ripple from his touch, and he bit his lip; it was stronger than he'd thought.

"I need your help." He turned to Cain who was desperately trying to hold Avery who was thrashing away, her eyes still wild as though she'd seen something terrifying. Which she most likely did, as Bastein's mom had probably cast a *fear* spell—which made the intruders see their darkest fear—on top of the magical barrier.

"Fine...*fine*..." Cain said hastily, performing a *legare* where it emitted spiky white particles.

A magical rope went towards Avery and tied around her, and Cain then did a quick *silenziare* where a wrapped tape appeared on Avery's mouth and all she did was make muffled, squealing noises.

After that, Cain then joined Bastein, and they stood in front of the barrier.

"*Dissolvere!*" the two of them chanted, and slowly but surely, a ripple was starting to take place on the barrier.

At first, it was stubborn, since the ripple would tear apart for a brief second before it closed again, which made the two Insians try again until finally, the ripple became bigger and bigger.

The spell eventually dissolved the barricade, which made the barrier shatter like glass, and pieces of the block twinkled down though they evaporated as soon as they touched the ground.

Cain panted. "Is that everything, or can we go in now?"

Bastein swiftly glanced at his mom's room, then after a few seconds, he nodded. "That should be it."

Avery squealed in protest as if to say "*don't forget about me!*"

"Looks like the fear spell has faded away." Bastein nodded.

Cain sighed. "Do we *have* to bring her?"

Avery squealed, nosily.

"Just bring her in," Bastein muttered.

After Avery had been set free, the three of them walked inside the study room which was medium-sized. Gothic architecture was definitely imprinted all over the place. Sleek, black bookshelves had been placed against the walls, and all of them were filled with books. The room was adorned with cathedral-like windows, tall and narrow, with a pointed arch and complete with stained glass.

It created an ethereal glow from the sun that shone at the panes. Rich, velvet curtains were draped against them, and there were old decors plastered everywhere, including on the mahogany desk that stood in front of the room, behind the windows. And the walls were painted with a black bean color.

The desk was topped with an old, green vintage lamp with a golden globe that spun around as though by magic. Cain ducked down when a book flew clumsily towards him before flying back up again.

"Some place," he said.

Avery smiled. "I missed coming here."

"Anyways...let's look for books that would have *Enoia*?"

The three of them got to work. Bastein decided to look at the flying books all over the room. Cain went to look at the shelves on the other side of the room while Avery looked at some other shelves, as well. They rummaged through as quick as they could, going as far as to even summon books on ancient languages, which ended up with no luck. Or at least, they thought they didn't have any luck.

"Anything?" Avery called out after a while.

"Nothing!" the boys answered.

She let out a frustrated sigh. They were losing time, and it probably wouldn't be too long before Sylvette would come running to her study room.

"*Portare Avanti!*" she shouted from frustration, and sure enough, a medium-sized black book came zipping through the air before it smacked her in the face. The boys sniggered.

Shaking her head, Avery smirked. "I found it!"

"You cheated." Bastein scowled.

The two boys then scurried towards her, and they all were huddled around one another as they flipped through the pages.

"Ah, ha! There! Lyaric!" Avery said, triumphantly.

On the page, there were strange symbols, and some of them looked similar to the letter.

Cain took the letter out of his pocket and started to match the symbols that were a star with a circle followed by a upside-down triangle then by a triangle with a circle around it and so on. He continued to match the symbols on the book as Avery performed another charm in which a floating scroll appeared out of thin air. A quill was furiously writing down the letters. She let out an exhausted sigh as she pulled out her pendant and noticed that at least half of her magic was nearly gone.

"You need to recharge soon," Bastein pointed out as he checked his ring, which wasn't as bad as Avery's.

She dismissed it, Bastein giving her a warning look.

"Avery—"

"Look! The quill wrote it down," she said, ignoring him. She grabbed the paper and began to examine it. Cain furrowed his eyebrows.

"So nothing...not much of an insight to this language."

Bastein sighed. "So, we're back to square one, then."

Avery shook her head. "No. Don't you *dare* give up, Bastein."

"Think about it, Avery! My parents and your grandpa won't tell us anything about this key or about this Uris Amos. Your grandpa is probably sending us on a wild goose chase." Bastein flared, annoyed at the situation. Annoyed at how they didn't seem to be getting anywhere.

"Listen, we're not giving up on this, okay? We can do this...without your parents' help. Look how far we have come already," Avery said. "And besides, I *might* know someone who might know these things."

Cain stared at her. "How do you know so much? What other secrets are you keeping?"

Avery rolled her eyes. "That secret? It's called shopping."

The two boys groaned.

"Listen," she insisted. "You know that man who runs the Antique shop at the Town Center? I bet you he would know about this stuff, or at least old things. He has an *antique shop!* Surely, he knows some things about the old."

Cain sighed. "Well...I suppose we could go and see...assuming he *would* tell us."

Avery shrugged. "What have we got to lose?"

Bastein was about to speak when he heard a voice that sounded like his mom. It seemed as though the other two heard it as well while he was panicking.

"My mom's coming!" he hissed.

"We have to hide!"

Avery gasped. "The melted lock!"

"No time for that now!" Cain whispered.

Cain quickly threw the book in the air so that it was floating once more before the three of them chanted "*essere inosservato*" and became invisible just in time as Sylvette looked at her study room with narrowed eyes. She knew she hadn't left the door open, and she looked around the floor...

There. The melted lock.

She cautiously stepped inside and sniffed the air.

Magic.

Smirking, Sylvette went back to her door after performing a spell, and then she locked it. After a while, the three became visible again, and they breathed out a sigh of relief.

"Did your mom seriously lock us in again?" Cain glared at him.

Bastein shrugged. "Probably."

He groaned as Avery squeaked.

"Uh, guys...I think we have a bigger problem."

"What?"

She helplessly looked down and gave a grimacing look. "We're sinking..."

CHAPTER TWELVE

THE AETHERAL KEY

"Your mom just had to pull a sinking spell, didn't she?" Cain moaned as he massaged his lungs after being painfully pulled out of the sinking hole. It was quite a chore to even get out of one.

Bastein rolled his eyes. "Well, none of this would've happened if you guys hadn't snuck into my mom's room."

Avery glared. "You were on this, too, *but—*" Her eyes sparkled with delight. "We got what we wanted! Cain, you still have that paper, right?"

He nodded, fishing out of his butt pocket to pull out that paper. "Right here."

"Great! Now, let's go to that Antique store."

"Sure, but first, you need to rest," Bastein warned her. "You look really pale."

AFTER RESTING—WHICH couldn't be done faster and made Avery happy—the three headed out to the town center to visit the Antique shop. Perhaps she could find some new décor...? She pulled out her pendant from her shirt and saw it was fully charged; she supposed it had come dangerously close to being emptied, but she *did* feel better, and hopefully no longer pale.

Upon arriving at the brown antique store, they noticed how busy it was. The store had brown wooden floor with beige walls, and the entire place was surrounded by many shelves in different sizes: tall, short, and medium. It was filled with antique items such as old clocks and typewriters—which Avery desperately wanted until Cain reminded her why they were here in the first place—and old chandeliers and pianos and so much more.

The store itself was two-storey high, with a staircase circling a portion of it. The three reached the tan counter right at the entrance where they could also see shelves behind the counter, filled with items that could only be bought if they had requested it.

Cain noticed the bell and decided to ring it for help. Sure enough, a tall, hairy man appeared from the crowd and scurried to the table. He had long grey hair with a long grey beard, and he had on half-spectacles that settled on his nose bridge. He wore a white, flowy blouse with black pants and boots, and around his neck was a necklace while on his right hand were several rings on different fingers.

"How may I help you?" he asked, pulling his spectacles up to his eyes until they widened in surprise. "Ah, Lockman. How do you do?" He motioned to Avery. "And you two might be?"

"They're my friends, Asgot. Cain and Bastein," she introduced them to him. The two boys nodded in acknowledgement.

Asgot was a Historical Linguist as well as a Paleologist. Avery remembered the first time she'd met him. She had thought him a nice person, always willing to help and to share his knowledge from his career.

Because she was close with Asgot—or used to be—he would let her go to restricted sections of the stores. And that was when she'd discovered a hidden trapdoor after tripping over an uneven rug. She'd merely opened the trapdoor due to curiosity and taken a short look, but she got in trouble when a furious Asgot appeared. From there, things had changed between them.

"That's good, that's good," he muttered. "Now...how can I help you?"

Avery looked around, and the crowd kept getting busier. She then lowered her voice, making Asgot have to strain his ears.

"Can we talk somewhere private?"

Asgot eyed the crowd and nodded. "Alton!"

A short, sturdy boy scurried towards the table. "Y-yes, sir?"

"Watch over the counter, will you? I've got some other business to deal with." He motioned to the three.

Alton nodded.

"Well, then, follow me," Asgot said.

The three entered his office though it looked very much like a storage shed since stacked boxes were spread throughout the room and around a small table at the back.

One thing Cain felt was how stuffy the room was and how everything seemed to be dusty as though it hadn't been cleaned in years, and he turned around to see Asgot closing the brown, torn curtains.

"Now then...erm...would you like to sit?" Asgot offered even though the room provided no chairs.

The three shook their heads.

"That's fine. Now, then, what would you like to discuss?"

Avery hesitated. She glanced at the two—Bastein pretended to be interested in the room while Cain gave a small nod where only Avery could see it. This was really their last chance to get some information since Avery knew her grandpa might not want to tell anymore *because* it might get too into their heads...he might not be wrong, in this case. She frowned. But why bother telling the story in the first place?

"Um...we were doing research for my grandpa. He told us a fairy-tale story. We thought it was fake at first until we decided to actually research further. Upon our research, we discovered this," she said and took out the paper from her jeans and showed the symbols.

She bit her lip, and the look on Asgot's face changed dramatically. It grew dark and tense, and he clenched his fists, turning his knuckles white.

"I'm sorry, but I know no such thing," he said instantly. "I'm very busy, and I need you three to move along."

The three gave a bewildered look to each other at the sudden change. "Wait, but we need to know—"

"I'm sure you do, but I *am* busy," Asgot interrupted Cain who closed his mouth.

Avery glared, tightening her own fists. She moved forward and dropped her voice to a whisper so that only she and Asgot could hear it. "I know what you're doing after hours...and if you don't want me to bring authorities, you'll tell us..."

Asgot's face grew stony, devoid of any emotions, but she knew he was slowly considering it. After all, with the business he had outside of his store, she could blackmail him and use it against him. He let out a slow breath.

"*Fine,*" he snarled quietly. He took step back, straightened himself, and turned around so that his back was facing them. He clasped both of his hands together behind his back and stared at his table.

"What you're seeking has been lost throughout history. No one, not after Uris Amos, has been able to find it. Some say he has taken in it to his grave which is located at the Kilhelm. Other says it just simply dissolved and is waiting to appear to the rightful owners. Or rather to the descendants of Uris Amos. And that—" he gestured to the symbols. "That is the Aetheral Key."

"But what exactly *is* the Aetheral Key?" Bastein asked.

Asgot turned around. "It has been said that the Aetheral Key is the key to unlock another world that has been forgotten by us. But that world has been sealed shut, and no one knows where the portal could be. Regardless, the Aetheral Key is made up by those relics that have been scattered. Those relics are said to be a dagger's handle, and a mirror. What kind of mirror and handle? No one really knows, but what we do know is that they cannot be ordinary items. But, be warned..." His tone suddenly went dark and ominous. "Those who find the Aetheral Key and unlock the forgotten world can bring chaos, especially if it falls into the wrong hands."

Bastein shivered.

"What kind of world?" Cain questioned.

"That...is the answer we do not have, but we could only imagine it."

"Say these relics existed. How do we know they are the ones? How would we know what they look like? And *where* would we get it?" Avery asked.

"You cannot just buy these relics. They have to *appear*. You will know because you'll sense immense power from them. A dagger's handle will only be shown if a truly great sacrifice was shown. For the mirror...well..." He stroked his beard. "In the books, they say the mirror can be used as a portal. That being said, the mirror *could* be summoned, but only with the right words and with the right location. What location, that is something you'll have to figure out."

There was a heavy feeling in the room which left less air to breathe, and if Cain had difficulty breathing earlier due to the stuffiness, he found it even harder now.

Avery let go of her breath. "Thank you, Asgot. This...helped us a lot..."

He glowered, but she made no expression.

"I'm glad," he simply said. "Now, off you go."

Nodding, the three started to go, but Asgot suddenly called out.

"Oh, and by the way, I must warn you. Should you go looking for these relics, many have gone insane and have been found dead."

With that, the three were ushered out of the room as Asgot watched them with his unnerving eyes.

CHAPTER THIRTEEN

KILHELM

Bastein shivered. "Man...he's a bit...unnerving. How does he know so much?"

They'd finally come back home, and the three of them were sitting in Bastein's room.

"He's a Historical Linguist and Paleologist who likes to dig in the past," Avery answered. "Regardless, we found what we need. Now, we just need to figure out how to get to Kilhelm."

"You're still thinking of pursuing this?" Cain asked quietly. He was the one who didn't get scared easily, but after that ominous note Asgot had left them with, he wasn't quite sure if he wanted to pursue this even further. He was positive nothing good would come out of this, and if anything, this might be a lose-win situation.

"I think it'll be a great adventure," Avery said enthusiastically. "Come on...when was the last time we had adventure like this?"

Bastein shuffled on his feet. "But you got to admit that this whole thing is quite literally under the rug and eerie. I don't know...something about this...it feels unsettling. We're chasing something that might not be real."

She sighed. "Okay...how about...we just go and hope for the best? If we find nothing at all, then we stop this journey and leave it as a ghostly tale."

Cain shook his head. "I don't know, and also, even if we all agreed to do this, how would we get to Kilhelm? It's north of Nothingsville, and that's way too far from here. It's about a two-day trip."

"Then, we have to convince the parents to let us go. We'll tell them that we're going to go to Warlord Wakeley—"

"You want us to *lie* to my parents and to your grandpa?" Bastein asked incredulously. "Avery."

"We're not lying. We're simply telling half of the truth, and even if we told them where we're going, they wouldn't let us."

"With good reason. Kilhelm is someplace where you *don't* wanna go," Cain said. "It's a forbidden place where people have *died*, Avery. By choice or no choice, and some say they could feel an evil presence. And besides, Warlord Wakeley doesn't even take a day to see all of the stuff. Five hours, at most."

"Probably because you could see Kilhelm from that desert," Bastein muttered.

Avery let out a frustrated groan. "Fine. We could rent out a hotel and stay there or something."

"That would be a waste of money."

"*Fine.* Then you chickens stay here, and I'll go myself," she said and got up.

"Wait," Bastein suddenly said as Avery was about to reach for the door knob. "We could stay at Esnet. It's a two-day trip and maybe...a few extra hours away from Kilhelm."

The three of them fell into silence as they were mulling over this idea. This could work, if everything went according to plan.

Avery watched the two of them; Cain seemed really quiet about this.

"Are you guys sure you want to go?" she asked quietly.

"Not really...but we don't have a choice, do we?" Bastein replied.

She nodded then turned her attention to Cain who had been staring at the floor with deep concentration.

"Cain?"

He shook his head. "I still think this is a bad idea, but I do agree with Bastein. We have to get to those items—assuming they exist. *But,* if they don't and this mission is a complete waste, we're dropping this fairy-tale."

Avery nodded, a huge smile etched onto her face. "It's a deal."

THE SOUND OF THE TRAIN calmed Avery as she rested her head against the cold window and let her thoughts go free. She was relieved the adults had agreed for them to go to Esnet, or at least that's what they thought. Regardless, she thought Esnet was actually a nice tourist attraction, and the main draw was that, even if the four seasons passed by, it will always be winter. One day, she'd go to it and see the place for herself.

"What do you think we'll find once we get to Kilhelm?" Bastein asked.

"Nothing but graves," Cain answered.

Bastein shivered.

What seemed like hours later, they finally reached Kilhelm while noticing they were the only ones left in their wagon.

"Kilhelm," the computerized voice announced, and the door slid open, which allowed them to exit. The train then allowed the doors to close before letting out a puff of smoke until it moved away, leaving the three in total silence. No one spoke or moved. They were simply staring ahead at a hill where they knew behind it lay the desert.

"Kilhelm," Cain announced almost quietly.

Ahead of them, they could see a large black gate surrounding the entire area, but there was most likely a magical barrier which would prevent people like the three of them to go in. Only high authorities may enter here.

"Are you sure this is really a grave?" Bastein asked with a nervous tone.

"Yes...I'm sure there are bodies buried beneath those crosses," Cain replied, making Bastein cringe.

Avery stood there numb, looking at the cloudy, gloomy weather that had befallen the land. But the weird thing was...she could've sworn she'd been here *before*. She was sure of it. She closed her eyes, allowing herself to look through her memories, to see if there were any signs of seeing this place before. She then opened her eyes.

"Hey, we've been here before, remember?" Bastein suddenly said, and he turned to Avery who came to the same conclusion.

"Yeah, I know..." she said quietly.

This was where she'd been found when they were playing the game. She just hadn't known what it was called.

Avery took a step back as thousands of memories of this place entered her mind from when she got attacked by that headless spider. Her heart was racing fast. Perhaps this wasn't a good idea.

She tentatively took a step towards the black gate, and she knew there was a magical barrier. Bastein looked around and noticed there was a rock, so he went towards it, picked it up, and threw it across the gate. The rock ended up being zapped by the invisible barrier.

"That's what I thought," Avery said. "There are security measures around this place. How are we going to destroy it?"

The security measures had been set up by the Congress of Magia as a means to protect the citizens simply because of what lurked in this place, and over time, the place had been forgotten.

"It wouldn't be as simple as it was with my mom's study room," Bastein pointed out. "If anything, the security would be *extra* tight."

Cain let out a breath. "So...should we try together? It might work."

Avery bit her lip. "It might, but...we should be careful so that we don't completely drain ourselves."

Cain nodded. "Right, then...on three?" They nodded. "One..." They all grabbed their hands together, squeezing them tightly, and they all closed their eyes. "Two..."

They all let their breaths out. "Three!"

They opened their eyes just as they said *"Diffondere!"*

A large, powerful blast of silver energies rushed towards the invisible barrier. *Diffondere* was the strongest version of *Dissolvere*, so it should work by breaking the wall. They felt themselves sliding backwards a bit as the force field bounced back their attack, refusing to dissolve, and it retaliated by being stubborn and not letting go of its protection.

Avery growled, feeling their power coming back at them, but she refused to lose. They had gotten this far, and she refused to go back. Her energy grew brighter, and her beam got stronger, which made her slide backwards a bit, but there, in a glimpse of an eye, a small ripple started to break through.

"We're doing it!" she yelled from all the chaos. "We need more power!"

All three silvery beams suddenly began to be bigger, stronger, and brighter, which illuminated the eerie place in an ethereal glow and eventually, the ripple in the force field started to grow and grow, until finally it...*exploded.*

The barrier shattered like glass, its pieces twinkling down like rain, but because of the explosion, it threw the three of them backwards, which made them land on the ground with a hard impact.

Avery winced as her palm scraped against the small rocks on the ground though she shakily pushed herself while the other two also followed suit.

"Everyone okay?" Bastein croaked, shaking.

Heavy breathing filled the air as they watched how fog suddenly appeared, but as it did, the gate opened by itself, which revealed the entrance.

Cain shook as he spoke. "This is it... *Kilhelm.*"

CHAPTER FOURTEEN

THE HIDDEN TOMB

Kilhelm used to be an active place, and it would be where all the sinners would go for their punishments. After being sent to the trials to see if they were guilty, the authorities would then drain their magic and put them here. Because of all the dead bodies, Kilhelm had now been infested with such dark and evil spirts.

Avery cautiously walked the ground of Kilhelm. Everything about this place was just so unsettling, and she couldn't believe she had been here before.

"By the way," she started. "When I was here, I remember seeing a temple, but it was locked. If we could find the key, maybe it'll open it up." Regardless, she didn't know since it was just a theory she had.

"Temple?" Cain frowned. "Why would there be a temple here?"

She shook her head. "I don't know, but that's what I just remembered now."

The three continued to walk in silence though the area around them didn't help as it was already silent, but as they did, Avery couldn't help but feel that something was calling to her. Something big. She's just wasn't sure what it was. Was it from this place? Could be. But she hated how this place was absolutely draining her, especially from all the evil energy she could feel.

Speaking of energy, she pulled out her pendant. It showed she had used a third of it; she still had a lot of magic.

"Hey, how's your magic?" she asked the two, and Cain checked his watch while Bastein checked his ring. They were all evenly matched.

"We used a third of it. Is it the same as you?" Bastein asked, and she nodded. "Good."

"Be careful. We really have to keep an eye on it," Cain warned.

They continued to walk, passing by endless hills of crosses. Avery wasn't sure what they were supposed to be looking for, but if anything, a tomb would be sufficient. Where *exactly* the tomb would be found, she didn't know, so they were mindlessly walking which she didn't really like, and also, she was sure security would show up at any minute, which could cause complications. They would have to avoid them so they wouldn't get caught.

The three went through the fog, but about halfway, Cain suddenly sensed something.

"Go right ahead..." He suddenly stopped as the two of them disappeared in the fog. "Thanks," he muttered.

He then swept his eyes across the area though it was hard to tell because it was so dark and the fog didn't really help, either.

"*Lux*," he muttered, and a flick of his hand emitted out a white glow. He continued to walk towards the foggy area—although he had noticed it was really foggy—until he suddenly saw a figure who seemed to crouch, hugging his knees. It looked like a child.

"Hello?" he asked cautiously. "Are you okay? Do you need help?"

He stopped. *Help.* Where was security? Shouldn't they be here because they'd opened the gate? He shook his head.

"Hey, kid...do you need help?" He also heard how the crying started to become louder.

A figure emerged from the shadows in front of the kid, and it seemed to be holding some kind of an object in its hand, but Cain couldn't make out what the object was because of all the mist

"Hey, watch it!" he warned and ran towards the boy until his cries stopped once Cain came closer to him.

The figure vanished, which made Cain blink. There *had been* a figure here, right?

"I could get you help and return you to your parents...but can you trust me?" he asked and placed his hand on the kid's shoulder.

Just like that, the crying stopped, which unnerved Cain. Something in his gut told him he should get away.

The minute he put his hand on the shoulder, all of a sudden, there was a small movement from the kid, and then, in a quick rapid movement, the figure suddenly turned his head where it let out a ghastly scream, its black eyes dripping with black tears. The second it opened its mouth, small bats flew out of it.

Yelping, Cain jumped back only to fall on the ground, and he quickly scrambled backwards while watching the figure crawling in a creepy manner.

His heart started to beat rapidly, and it felt like it was going to break his ribs, though while in the midst of the creepy crawler, he also noticed something started to come out from the piles of crosses surrounding him—something black that resembled water.

Streams of black water started to seep from the ground, and Cain hastily scrambled up in attempt to get away. But the black water was just too quick for him, and it enveloped his legs, trapping him so he couldn't get away. It felt as though his legs were enclosed in cement, making it impossible to move his legs.

"Get it off me!" he yelled before placing his hand on the cement-like black water where he shouted out a fire spell. "*Flarego!*"

A streak of red fiery fire burst from his hand, and it ignited the black water in flames, causing it to also rush towards the creepy crawler which got struck by the attack.

It screamed something awful which made Cain clamp his ears shut, and he watched the fieriness of it all as the crawler got engrossed in flames. It screeched before it rushed towards Cain who put his hands up in front his face, feeling the breeze of the creature passing by.

He then looked back as the creature vanished, but as it did, it seemed as though it cleared up the area just a bit since Cain could manage to see a fallen angel statue with wide open arms, but the face seemed sad.

He stared at the angel before he shivered at the creepy feeling of the statue and then he ran.

But just as he was about to start running, he suddenly felt the ground shaking with such big tremors, he thought the earth would split open.

His breath quickened from the unexpected call, and he anxiously looked back and forth and above, and there, amidst the fog, he was able to see four yellow, glowing eyes. He gasped and quickly hid himself against the crosses while watching the seven-foot creature resembling a gargoyle that stomped through the earth, making it shiver upon its impact.

Security was here.

✕✕

"CAIN!? CAIN!" AVERY yelled.

The two of them suddenly realized Cain had gone missing when they wanted to ask him a question. However, they were met with silence, and that was when they recognized he wasn't with them.

"Where could he have gone?" Bastein asked worriedly.

"I don't know."

"Cain!"

"Wait...something's coming," Bastein warned. "Get ready."

Avery stood her ground as she looked around for the intruder Bastein had mentioned. It grew bigger and bigger until she panicked and started to attack.

"*Flarego!*"

"*Aqualis!*"

"*Barrius!*"

Multiple lights sparked the area, and the two's attacks bounced off to the side from the shield that was created.

"Will you guys stop?!"

Bastein raised an eyebrow. "Wait...Cain?"

The figure walked out of the fog, revealing a battered-up Cain, though what shocked Avery the most was that he looked *shaken*.

"What happened—"

"Nothing," he abruptly interrupted her.

"Nothing? We looked *everywhere* for you, Cain!" Bastein yelled. "How could you say nothing? Where *were* you? What *happened* to you?!"

"Shh," he said abruptly. "We got bigger problems to worry about. Security is here."

The two suddenly shook with dread. They had heard about the security in here—giant seven-foot creatures with glowing, yellow eyes were rumored to roam around these places to make sure nothing got out.

Avery grimaced. "Where are they?"

"Just down that way." Cain motioned with his head. "They're not far from here, and we're going to be in a lot of trouble. So, we better hurry up and find that tomb."

Bastein frowned and looked around the area where it seemed clear. No more hills of crosses, but it was still covered up in fog.

"So, how do we know if we have found it? Like, are we actually looking for a tomb or something else? Because I don't see this place would have graves." He shook his head. "We don't know, but we might think it's an actual tomb."

Cain looked around the area once more, and he noticed how it split up into three different pathways that could either lead to the crypt or to death, and after what he had just experienced, he didn't want to take any chances. Regardless, he still proposed an idea.

"How about we split up? There are two different pathways. I know, not the greatest idea, but it's the best chance we got. We don't have much time since we got security on our tails, and should we run into any problem, just shoot out sparks, okay?"

The two mutely nodded.

"Then, we'll go at the temple as our final destination." Bastein suggested, and they all agreed.

"Right...well, good luck."

"DO YOU THINK WE'LL find it?" Bastein asked as they roamed around the path.

Cain shrugged. "Perhaps, but we need to worry about the security. I've seen one of them. I'm sure there's more."

Bastein sighed. "Fantastic."

Nonetheless, the two roamed around the pathway though it wasn't until halfway during their trip that Cain stopped walking as he suddenly felt a tremor that shook the earth. He looked up and noticed the same bright light he had witnessed when he came here. Eyes wide, he quickly pulled Bastein away from sight and hid behind a pile of crosses nearby.

He pointed up to the light, and Bastein formed an *o* before he clamped his mouth shut. The security.

"How are we going to avoid it?" Bastein whispered.

Cain shook his head. He didn't have a clue, but he could only hope it wouldn't spot them. Regardless, he lowered his voice to a whisper as the security could hear voices. However, they were partially deaf to lowered ones.

Regardless, there might be a chance where they would have to fight it if they weren't careful, and Cain hoped it wouldn't have to come down to that.

"Quietly...we have to go around it, and whatever you do, avoid the light. Do *not* get caught. Understood?"

Bastein mutely nodded, fearful for his life. Cain took a breath and scanned the area, looking out for the guard. It shouldn't be too hard to miss as it had a gigantic light on it which was a dead giveaway. Spotting that it was straight ahead—which was the direction they needed to go—he motioned quietly so Bastein could follow him, and the two of them went into stealth mode.

"Couldn't we use the invisibility spell?" Bastein asked quietly

Cain shook his head. "They would sense magic, and we would be an easy prey because of it. The less we use magic, the better. And besides—" he checked his watch. "We shouldn't be using too much of it."

The two stalked the night, dodging left and right while there was an occasion where they hid behind the piles of crosses before they would be able to make a move again.

Everything seemed to be going according to plan until Bastein accidentally tripped over a cross and clumsily fell over, hitting the floor. The guard stopped walking and turned around.

Cain roughly pulled Bastein up, and they hid in the pile. None of them breathed while the guard was scanning the area until a few minutes had passed, and they let out a long-exhaled breath.

"Really?" Cain hissed.

"It's dark," Bastein shot back. "We have no light other than the guard's light."

Nevertheless, the two resumed their walking while being more cautious than before. They couldn't make the same mistake twice; they were lucky they'd had the pile since the deeper they went, it seemed as though the piles kept getting farther and farther away from them. They could no longer use them to their advantage.

But the more they kept walking, Bastein couldn't help but feel that something was following them. Was it another security? He didn't know, although he hoped it wasn't.

Right there, he should've trusted his instincts for something *was* following them, slithering on the ground as it was heading towards them. Sure, it may be a vine, but they could be deadly. They were poisonous. And then, it suddenly wrapped itself around Bastein's ankle, which made him scream as he, without a warning, fell to the floor and was suddenly being dragged to the darkness.

"Cain! HELP!" he screamed.

"Bastein!"

Because of the sound, it made the guard stop moving and turn its stone head towards the noises, which made Cain pause.

"Oh, no," he moaned.

Acting quickly, he rushed towards Bastein who was trying to fight it off while also running away from the security who was charging at them by *flying* towards them. The great monstrous wings were all Cain heard as it came closer and closer.

"*Ardenti igne!*" Bastein exclaimed as a ball of fire came from his mouth and it burned the vines who screamed from pain before they were burnt to ashes.

Panting, Bastein stood there, feeling frazzled though he heard footsteps which made him scramble the other way.

He was about to use a spell though he cancelled it in time when he heard Cain.

"Bastein! Bastein!"

Cain came into view, and he stopped, panting though he didn't have a second to lose since he remembered the guard was coming for them.

"Get up, you fool. Because of the noise, the security is coming for us!"

Cain harshly pulled Bastein up, and they started to run away from the gargoyle who was flying at them at an incredible speed. Frantically, Bastein summoned spells that could maybe leave at least a mark on the gargoyle while Cain also performed spells to attack back.

The gargoyle was too fast for them, and it kept dodging the oncoming attacks, left and right before it swooped down towards the boys who jumped to the side to avoid being caught.

Cain narrowed his eyes as he saw the creature making a U-turn before it came back again, and he glared at the light. He got up, rushing towards the creature, and shouted out a spell.

"*Exstinguo!*"

A blast of red energy zapped through the air, and it struck true since it had hit the light which got extinguished, engulfing them in darkness. The creature screamed in pain, and it clumsily flew down, crashing on the ground with a hard thud.

Dust and debris flew out, and Cain rushed towards Bastein, producing a magical barrier around them, protecting them from the rocks.

Unfortunately, that wasn't enough to stop the creature since it was still getting up, still determined to destroy its prey, though the only thing putting it at a disadvantage was that it had no light, and it couldn't see where the prey was.

Without waiting, the beast started to attack at random which made the two dodge left and right. The blast would hit the piles which made them fly in the air from the impact, and it scratched at Bastein's cheek, which made him wince.

Bastein started to run from the oncoming attack, but Cain grasped his hand tightly and stared at him, forming a plan in his mind.

"Together. It's the only way we could beat him with fire attacks," he said.

"You think it'll work?"

"What do we have to lose?"

Nodding, Bastein stood his ground, determination flashing across his mind, and together, they unleashed the fire attack.

"*Ardenti igne!*"

The large ball of fire streak rushed out of their mouths and swirled around each other before it emerged together, creating a bigger wave. It swirled around and around until it struck the creature's attack with full force, and for the time being, it seemed like a tug of war with one side decreasing, and then it would be the opposite.

Until at last, the fire streak devoured the light-blue energy, and it shrank more and more until it finally struck the beast who let out a shrill of agony before it exploded. The rocks flew everywhere, and Cain was quick enough to perform a magical barrier around them until it had subsided.

Once he was sure it was safe, he lowered the barrier, and the two of them fell to their knees, exhausted. They were trying to catch their breaths since they had used quite a large amount of magic in order to defeat such a beast.

"What a hündin," Cain muttered as they got up.

SO FAR, AVERY HATED this place. It was dark, cold, and creepy, and it didn't help how the fog was covering everything to the point where her light charm wasn't even illuminating the place properly. But she was scared to use up all her magic; she needed to conserve it. She needed to be smart about this, especially since they got security. She hoped they hadn't seen them.

Nonetheless, she continued to trek down the straight path though when she had entered the place, she had been feeling weird about it. Something was calling to her, and she didn't know what it was. It was strange and creepy, but she couldn't tell if the calling was a good one or an evil one.

"*Avery...*" a voice suddenly called, which made her stop.

She'd just...imagined it, right? She shook her head and resumed walking.

"*Avery...*"

The voice grew louder.

"Who's there?" she said with a sharp tone.

"Why are you like that? Follow us!"

And there, ahead, stood a figure which made her take a step back. It was hard to tell who it was due to the mist. However, it seemed as though the figure only watched her before it flew away, vanishing from sight.

"Wait!" she called out, running after the silhouette.

She continued to follow the figure until she entered a new area, one that seemed to have too much mist. However, she stopped running and saw the figure standing far from her.

"Who are you?" she shouted.

Sploosh.

Avery frowned and looked down where something dull was gleaming beneath her. Water? She was confused, though she looked up to still see the figure there.

"Wait!"

She ignored the water that seeped into her shoes as she ran towards the figure, but when she seemed close to it, the shadow suddenly vanished along with its fog. And there, it revealed something that looked like *tombs.*

Avery gasped, taking a step back from the unexpected view which made her shiver, but what was in front of her was even more shocking.

CHAPTER FIFTEEN

AN EVIL WISP

Avery gasped as she saw the grave. There was a skull laid right at the top of the bones from its arms, and the gaze was looking at her as though saying 'you awakened me?' She shuddered; she had heard before that those who opened curse crypts would be cursed, but she hoped she wouldn't be.

"It's the tomb," Bastein said after a long silence.

Cain and Bastein had finally caught up to her after the two of them had decided to face off the security while she was searching for the grave. The two boys arrived with bruises and bloody cuts with some parts of their clothes torn apart.

"Well, it's *a* tomb. Who's to say it belongs to Uris Amos?" Cain muttered.

"Inlucesco," Avery summoned, and a silvery light was made in the form of a ball around her hands.

The silvery light illuminated the area, and they were able to see the skull and the crossbones that were laid out in front of them, revealed from the broken coffin. Somebody had smashed the grave. But why? Had they been looking for something? Or had it been always like this?

After more examining, Avery found words etched across the tomb, following the arch of it.

Obdormabo in aeternum, donec excitant me semen meum.

"The words...what do they mean?" she asked, but none of them had any answer.

"So...would anyone like to raid a tomb?" Cain asked after a while.

Shivering, Avery made towards the coffin and crouched down to see something dull and glimmering from the light exposure. It was the key. The key was made from a skeleton bone laid on top of the crossbones.

"The key," she breathed.

She grabbed it and examined it. It seemed to be a regular key with intricate designs where the top resembled a time clock with gears etched into the metal. The two handles that stuck from the side resembled skeleton fingers while the blade was made from a skeleton bone.

Bastein breathed out a sigh of relief. "Oh, thank Mercy. Now, let's go back to the temple before things come...back."

Avery nodded. She stuffed the key into her pocket as the three of them began to walk away.

But as she turned, she suddenly heard dark, ill-omened voices.

Avery...Avery...

She stopped what she was doing and turned around, scanning the area before she shook her head and briskly walked to join the boys.

They eventually reached the temple, but the voices which Avery had heard previously grew stronger. She gritted her teeth as she tried to block them out, feeling shaken, and she shook her head.

No. Get out of my head.

"...Avery...are you okay?" Bastein asked, concerned.

She blinked and wearily looked up at the two boys who were staring at her with worry across Bastein's face.

"I'm fine..." she said through a smile. She then eyed the locked door and put on a determined look. "I'll open the door. I do have the key."

The two boys shuffled to the side as she approached the door. With a nervous hand, she fumbled in her pocket for the skeletal key and lifted it towards the hole.

Almost at once, the hole seemed to pulse with an eerie sapphire glow, and with a hard tug, Avery let out a gasp when the key started to wriggle in her gasp. Surprised, she let go of the key that began to float towards the hole that was a perfect fit.

And at once, there was a sharp click before the key let out a bright yellow color which forced the three to shield their eyes from the light. The lock groaned as it turned around and around before it clicked, indicating it got unlocked before the lock magically unclasped itself from the chain and fell to the floor with a loud thump.

The doors protested until they finally gave in and magically opened, which revealed a dark staircase leading down. Avery felt herself breathing quicker, but the minute the door was opened, she heard those same voices again. However, this time, she felt herself going in a trance after looking in the dark for a while.

Something compelled her to walk down, and she didn't hesitate. The two boys exchanged a look, shrugging before they followed her.

—✦—

AVERY...AVERY...

Veni ad me...Veni ad me...

The haunting whispers seemed to taunt Avery as she blindly followed them, obeying their command.

"This...feels dark..." Bastein said nervously as he looked around the dark blue temple where ancient words seemed to be around everywhere.

They finally reached the final step, and there, ahead of them, stood a dark purple sword with matching color for the gem in the black handles. It stuck straight down to the ground as though it was sealed solid, unable to escape from its prison. Around the sword were black chains tied securely to the weapon, which made it impossible for it to escape even if it wanted to.

Avery...Avery!

The voices seemed louder and impatient the minute Avery reached the sword, staring at it with a trance-like gaze.

"Is that...smoke around it?" Bastein asked, suspiciously.

A black mist surrounded the sword, and it seemed to pulse bigger and bigger, emitting out voices that only Avery could hear.

*Dimittite me et dabo tibi quod maxime placet...*the melancholy voice whispered.

"Yes..." she whispered.

Entranced, she walked towards the sword while the boys were examining the extended chains belonging to it.

"I don't like this," Bastein said again.

"I know...this place gives me the creeps," Cain muttered. His whole body tingled, feeling unwelcomed, and he turned around to see Avery walking towards the sword. However, he gasped as he saw what she was about to do, and he called out.

"Avery, no!"

But it was too late. Avery said the releasing spell before Cain could even warn her on time, and she touched the chains where it lit on fire and forced her to shield her eyes from the spell. The fire swallowed up the chains, rattling them against the impact of the incantation, and the black mist that once surrounded the blade engulfed the entire temple in the same black smoke.

At this point, Avery snapped herself out of it and shook her head, stepping back a bit as she wearily gazed around, trying to understand what was happening.

The smoke eventually cleared up since it was being pulled back to the sword like gravity, and the weapon started to take shape with the mist following its every move. The smoke cascaded down like a waterfall until, eventually, it revealed a figure

A grotesque, skeletal figure which the three laid their eyes upon.

Gasping, Avery tumbled backwards as the mist continued to form the figure. And the smell grew stronger and unbearable—sulfur and ashes combined together was something she wished she'd never have to smell again. The smell of death drifted throughout the room, and it made her dizzy.

She gasped as something hard tugged on her elbow.

"What did you do?!" Cain exclaimed.

Eyes wide, she shook her head. "I don't know! I don't remember!"

"What do you mean, you don't—"

"Guys, look—" Bastein whimpered, pointing to the scene.

A grotesque shadow had finally begun to take shape after the mist had subsided. The skeletal figure with hollow, socket eyes and a black torn cape that covered its skeletal body—though they were still able to see ribs poking out—didn't move, and it was still bent down as though it was bowing, but not to the three who were too speechless to do anything.

After a while, the figure straightened itself, and its two translucent sapphire blue eyes stared at them with a disturbing look where one would want to glance away but couldn't.

The three stared at the intruder who seemed to be looking at them with interest before it let out a demonic smile that made Cain turn around.

"Hello, my children," he whispered in a raspy, scratchy voice. He stared at the three with a wide smile before his eyes landed on Avery who stood there, frozen as she was unable to look away.

"You, my little one. Thank you for releasing me from my prison. I have spent over three hundred years in that vile confinement, but now that I'm finally free...I can return to my mission."

Avery shook her head, denying that she was the one responsible for releasing him...whoever he was.

"Who...who are you?" Bastein croaked in fear.

A smile escaped his lips so wide that Bastein thought for sure it would have split open his face. The second he said his name, Bastein instantly regretted for it was a name that would be engraved into their minds forever.

It was a name everyone would speak of for the destruction it would bring.

It was a name the citizens would mumble in fear.

It was a name that would bring a curse to the world.

He chuckled. "I am...Romanhalth."

ACKNOWLEDGEMENTS

And so begins a new series! I am so excited for this series that I have already started to plan my third book. A *lot* of research went into this. And, I'm so excited to start this series! However, I bet you're all dying to know what Draugur from Eventide had wanted from Avery. Well, I can only say wait until book six. Trust me...it'll make sense...or...if you really want to know, you can have your own theories with some research of the name Draugur. I'll give you a hint; it's from Old Norse.

Firstly, thank you to my editor Zee Monodee who continues to stick by my side who always gives out helpful feedback even though in return, I give her strange words where I'm sure she shakes her head, haha. Thank you!

Thank you to my beta-reader, Holly Mathewson, for being the best beta who always points out great plot holes and suggestions where it makes me think. Thank you!

Thank you to my dad who continuously reads my stories, giving out tips and tricks to make the story even better.

Thank you to my friend, Nyala Chaudary, who gave unique ideas to the story and is always excited to read new stories! Thank you!

Lastly, thank you to my readers for their continuous support and for giving me a chance to share my stories. Your support means everything to me!